A Bit of Christmas Whimsy

A BIT OF CHRISTMAS WHIMSY

A NOVELLA

DAVID EDMAN

Illustrated by Michael Carpenter

Publishing House
St. Louis   London

Concordia Publishing House, St. Louis, Missouri
Concordia Publishing House Ltd., E. C. 1
Copyright © 1974 Concordia Publishing House

MANUFACTURED IN THE UNITED STATES OF AMERICA

Library of Congress Cataloging in Publication Data

Edman, David.
    A bit of Christmas whimsy.

    I. Title
PZ4.E234Bi [PS3555.D57]   813'.5'4   74-6474
ISBN 0-570-03234-2

For Sarah

PRELUDE

Have you ever considered the whimsy involved in that very first Christmas gift of all? I mean, specifically, the manner in which it was given. Not that the gift itself was entirely whimsical. It was, more or less, what we'd always needed.

But the wrapping of it! Mere wood and straw. It was as though the fragility of the thing had something to do with it, truth being exceedingly fragile. Yet surprising, wouldn't you say? A deceptive bit of packaging for such a lavish gift.

And the surroundings! All that braying and mooing. Even cackling, I wouldn't be surprised. And that amoniacal barnyard odor. And the rustics barging in. And the sounds of revelry from next door.

Really, the entire episode was engineered in a most whimsical manner. So much so, that one is led to suspect a sort of divine humor behind it all.

A surprising idea, perhaps. And more surprising still when one considers that, if this be so, there remains the possibility of a fundamental merriment under everything that exists — everything, everything, everything.

One could even suppose that the molecules dance to some cosmic gigue, that the chromosomes form a garland about some quintessential joy, and that beyond the rim of space there abides an eternal good laughter which promises, as Juliana did, that all at last will be well.

I do not know if this be so. You will pardon me, I trust, for saying that I should certainly like to *think* it so. And, indeed, why should it *not* be so? Why not joy at bottom instead of darkness? Are not the scales, when all has been placed on them, tipped that way? Is it so difficult to suppose that the pangs and the tears — yes, and even the shudders of death itself — are but passing illusions, brief inexplicable pauses in some vast and joyous symphony? Is it so impossible to proceed on the assumption that the jars and jolts which attend life, are, in truth, the inconsequentialities, are mere momentary discords in some splendid and everlasting harmony?

You might reply that this is devoutly to be wished but hardly to be believed. And I would concur in that judgment.

Still, joy has a way of overtaking us, and it often does so in the most whimsical fashion. Why is it that a man, with no claim in the world to happiness, suddenly, unaccountably finds his heart uplifted? His business has failed. His wife has left him. A persistent and inexplicable pain gnaws at his innards. He fears the worst. Yet, despite all this and more, he suddenly finds himself positively ecstatic, finds he can barely repress the urge to dance and shout and go skipping down the staid streets of his neighborhood like a dervish. Why? Why, I say, unless it be that happiness is rooted at the very core of things and persists in dogging our sad footsteps and leaping out at us at the most inopportune moments?

Speaking of these possibilities, I've heard it suggested on very sound authority that this emergent whimsy becomes unusually active around the time of the winter solstice. Just when everything seems dreariest, there comes a virtual eruption of joy, bringing with it suggestions of a divine insistence that we rest us merry.

Count upon it, say those who know more about these things than I, Christmastide is the time when heaven forces its joy upon us. Not directly, to be sure. But in a roundabout fashion, through an unconscionable assortment of pranks and wiles.

No wonder we mislabel packages and tuck greeting cards into wrong envelopes. No wonder we spend too much on some barely tolerable nephew, yet manage to forget our next-to-oldest friends entirely. It's all due to that same Christmas whimsy which used a shed for the grand entrance.

So you must beware as Christmas draws nigh, say proponents of this unusual theory. Beware how you select your gifts and to whom you assign them, lest you find yourself the hero of some comedy in which you never really cared to play.

Beware also of how you receive your gifts. Heaven, they tell us, has a way of booby-trapping them, so that what initially seems so splendidly appropriate has a way of turning to ashes in our hands, while that plainly wrapped, bargain basement affair from some dragon of an aunt has a way of showering us with happiness for years to come.

Be chary, in other words. Give cautiously. Receive discerningly. Else heaven may have fun with you.

All of this puts me in mind of a story. It is not a long story. Nor is it noticeably profound. It is certainly not one of those three-deckered affairs with a lot of symbolism on the bottom, a bit of a plot on top, and heaven-knows-what in between. It is simply a tale of how two similarly wrapped Christmas gifts, from two quite different types of Fifth

Avenue shops, came to provide three persons — utter strangers to one another — with what were the most appropriate and joyous gifts they ever received, though none realized it at first.

Unfortunately, the story has more than its share of surprising turns and astounding coincidences, and I do feel under obligation to offer some explanation. This I have chosen to do by ascribing the entire affair neither to fate nor to chance, but rather to that very Christmas whimsy which I personally find myself too timid to believe and too terrified to deny.

HARLEM

The story begins on a Christmas Eve which took place many years ago during the presidency of that World War II hero of benign countenance.

All that day the men at the weather bureau had been predicting snow. Their self-congratulatory assurances of a white Christmas had been carried by radios to every corner of the city. Yet at four-thirty in the afternoon the thermometer still rested well above the point of freezing and not a flake in sight.

About this time a lad by the name of Rosie left a fifth-floor, cold-water flat in order to buy a most special Christmas gift. The tenement in which Rosie lived was located on 117th Street near Lexington Avenue. The nearest bus stop lay three blocks away, and it was there that Rosie directed his footsteps.

At this hour there was very little daylight left. Not that it mattered, for this was, after all, Manhattan, where there was no shortage of artificial illumination.

A low-pressure weather system lingered over the city. It had brought a cold rain around noon, which later evolved into a fine descending mist. As a result the streets of the city glistened. Lights, especially the little colored cones of Christmas tree lights — blues and reds and greens and yellows emanating from the windows of shop and apartment — shone as brightly from pools of water along the sidewalks as from their original source. Automobiles, brilliant with wetness, hissed along with that peculiar sound which comes of the combination of tire rubber and asphalt and rain.

Rosie shivered a little as he waited for the bus. His jacket was several sizes too small for him, exposing his wrists to the humid cold. At the same time his trousers, as if to compensate for the jacket, were too long. Their cuffs overlapped the heels of his tennis shoes and tended to blot up the water on the sidewalk, a process which tended to make his ankles as uncomfortable as his wrists, or perhaps even a little more so.

He was an ordinary sort of lad, Rosie. Neither very good nor very bad. Not highly intelligent, but not stupid either. He was the pride of his mother, but an occasional source of humiliation too. He yelled with other boys rounding corners. He disliked school. He performed favors generously, but duties grudgingly. And, when summoned by a call from his mother, he often pretended to be hard of hearing.

A brown leatherette cap with a bill was perched on his compressed black hair. His face beneath was common to his race — shallow eyesockets, a flat abbreviated nose, generous lips. His facial expression, when in repose, was one of utmost seriousness, even though Rosie was no more or less serious than most 11-year-old boys.

After a time a bus swerved toward the curb. It dispersed a puddle of water into two even splashes, then stopped, as New York City buses tend to do, with a curious wrenching noise in its rear end.

Rosie, along with one or two others, boarded. He paid for his fare by reaching into his jacket pocket and producing a tightly folded pair of dollar bills. These he unfolded until, in their innermost square, he came upon a small uneven column of coins, from which he selected two. These he dropped into the driver's coin box. The driver banged a lever, causing the box to swallow the coins with a clatter and digest them with irregular whirring noises.

Rosie then found a seat on the sidewalk side of the bus. He refolded the two dollar bills around the remaining coins and placed the wad into his jacket pocket, holding it there with his hand. For awhile he examined the faces of his fellow passengers. Then he directed his attention to the concave placards overhead, which advertised loans and spirits and lingerie.

Rosie's destination was not far off, though in one sense it was the other side of the world. He was bound for that most fantastic of all the world's shopping districts, Manhattan's Fifth Avenue. Here, with his accumulated funds, he intended to buy a Christmas gift for his mother. The rest of his Christmas shopping — mainly for two younger sisters, mainly candy, had been purchased locally. But his mother, he felt, deserved something far more special.

Rosie's request to take a trip downtown had been granted with considerable reluctance by his mother. She feared the effect that darkness had on the streets of New York, a darkness which had taken her husband from her and now continually threatened her son. But still she let him go. His heart was set on it. So she let him go. Let him go with the promise that he return by eight o'clock, in time for a late supper, a bath, and early bed, for on the morrow the family was bound for Aunt Mary's in Jersey City for a holiday celebration.

At 59th Street Rosie stepped through the ill-tempered

doors of the bus. He walked west, then, until he reached the corner of 59th and Fifth Avenue.

He dodged a few pedestrians as he turned the corner. Then suddenly he stopped. He looked. He stared. He gaped, as though he could scarcely believe what his eyes were taking in. For there, spread out before him, lay the most glorious vision he had ever beheld — the which, in point of fact, was nothing more than Fifth Avenue in its Christmas decor.

Rosie gazed enthralled down the length of the avenue, convinced that he had never seen anything quite so wonderful in his entire life. He had visited Fifth Avenue before, to be sure, during daylight hours, and it had seemed splendid to him even then. But now at night, with the holiday season at its crest, with the graceful lines of thousands and thousands of incandescent bulbs in a repeating sequence up and down the corridor of his sight, Fifth Avenue was Fifth Avenue no longer, but rather an utterly celestial thoroughfare filled with all of the munificence of heaven and earth, and laid out at his feet as though miraculously created for him and for him alone at this very instant.

The people rushing by looked immensely prosperous and happy to Rosie. He caught them between the glow of office parties and those last-minute purchases for which one spends money with such reckless buoyancy. Their laughter, their fragmented greetings and farewells, infected him with worldly joy, and for just a few moments he was content to do nothing more than listen to the sounds of human pleasure as they mingled with traffic noises and policemen's whistles and recorded music blaring from outdoor speakers.

Rosie spent most of the next two hours looking at window displays. He gazed upon them until surfeited. He looked at toys. He looked at candy. He looked at dummy Santas waving woodenly from laden sleighs. He watched mechanical elves pounding monotonously in chaletlike workshops. He gazed upon suspended angels festooned with costume jewelry. He even saw a wise man in the process of opening a treasure chest full of men's toiletries. It was all marvelous!

Time, however, soon began to press in upon him. As yet Rosie had not come upon anything for his mother which matched both his fancy and his means. He had stood for nearly half an hour before a store window filled with a lethal array of pocket knives and kitchen knives and hunting knives and scissors and clippers and other such implements all shining silver and steel against a red velvet background. But all of these items crammed together — their sheer number, their very proximity to each other having the effect of drawing attention — were one by one judged by Rosie to be either inappropriate or too expensive.

It was getting on toward seven o'clock when Rosie reached 42d Street. The crowds were sparser now, and in stores clerks could be seen idly talking to one another.

About this time Rosie came upon a man dressed in a Santa Claus costume. The man was standing by a red cardboard chimney protruding from the sidewalk. He gripped a bell with his right hand, which he incessantly clanged with the motion of one wielding a hammer. On an impulse Rosie unfolded his dollar bills, extracted a nickel, and dropped it down the chimney.

The Santa Claus winked at him. Rosie paid no attention, however. It further escaped his attention that a strange light

17

enfolded the two of them at this moment of impulsive generosity, nor did he hear the faint echoes of hosannas, for Rosie's mind had become preoccupied once more with the matter of a Christmas gift for his mother.

GREENWICH VILLAGE

The last time Jimmy had provided himself with that form of sustenance by which he chose primarily to live these days had been at 11 that morning. At that time he had injected a measured amount of heroin into one of the veins which ran under the skin of his inner left arm.

From then until one o'clock he had dozed and dreamed, then suddenly awakened to the realization that his supply of glassene envelopes, each with its pinch of white powder, was quite gone, that a holiday was just about upon him, and that he was utterly without funds to secure more.

The thought of it roused him at once. He set off for a coffee shop near Sheridan Square, where his most recent supplier customarily did business. But, when he arrived, the pusher was not there.

In the course of looking about for him, the young man ran into a fellow customer, a gypsy-looking girl named Deanna. She was something of a Village character, noted for the variety of large, enormously complex brass earrings which she wore, earrings which she had once made and been unable to sell.

Jimmy called out to her. However, before he could ask her where the pusher was, she asked him.

It occurred to him then that the pusher had been taken in by the police. Jimmy promptly forgot him and began

20

wondering what his next move ought to be. Almost at once his thoughts were drawn to a man he knew only as Sherm.

Sherm had been his first dealer and, by any standard of comparison, the best. So long as Jimmy had possessed the necessary money, Sherm had provided an unending supply of heroin. Thousands of dollars had passed from the young man's hands into the pockets of Sherm. But eventually Jimmy had run out of funds, then credit — the consequence being that he'd been forced to deal elsewhere.

Given the present predicament, however, Jimmy felt that it might not be a bad idea to try Sherm one more time. Sherm, after all, was one of the few gentlemen in the trade, or so he believed. More important, Sherm himself was not an addict. The type of pusher who was a user of his own product was usually broke and demanded cash. But Sherm was not in this particular mold. Sherm was a businessman. Sherm possessed capital. Sherm had no bad habits save for a slight addiction to money. Besides, Sherm's goods were always of the highest quality. Sherm believed customer satisfaction to be one of the first principles of sound business practice, and as a result he sold nothing but the best.

Fifteen minutes later Jimmy was walking back and forth in front of a basement antique shop on west Eighth Street. As he looked over the iron railing to the display windows below the level of the sidewalk, he wondered what his chances with Sherm might be. The last time he had seen Sherm, now some six weeks before, he had been told that his account was long overdue and that there would be no more purchases on credit.

Those who dealt with Sherm knew that here was a man who measured his words. Sherm was not the sort given to making idle statements. So at that time the young man had accepted his pronouncement as being as final and irrevocable as the laws of the Medes and the Persians which changeth not, and did not press for further credit.

But on this Christmas Eve afternoon there seemed no alternative but to try to persuade Sherm to extend his credit just one more time. What he needed, Jimmy realized, was a story — a good story to accompany his request.

As he paced the sidewalks there in front of Sherm's place, a certain possibility came to Jimmy's mind. He began to develop it. He worked on its plausibility. He touched up its consistency. He heightened its credibility. He closed its loopholes. He honed its logic. He broadened its overall pathos. He raised questions about the story and answered them. He formed objections and countered them.

Finally, goaded both by a gathering desperation and a firm faith in his own ability to be convincing, he descended the concrete steps and entered the empty shop to the ting-a-ling of a bell set ringing by the opening door.

The young man passed through a haphazard array of dusty furniture, lamps, and bric-a-brac to a curtained-off room in the back. Here he found Sherm working at his roll-top desk.

"Hi, Sherm," he said in as engaging a manner as he could muster.

Sherm looked up.

"Well, well, well, well, well," Sherm said, and he leaned far back in his chair. The shift of his weight — and he was a heavy man — caused the desk chair to tilt backwards to the accompaniment of the sound of spring steel being stretched.

"Look who's come to see us," Sherm went on. "Our old friend Jim. Got a Christmas present for us, I bet."

All of this was being spoken to a heavyweight adolescent named Leonard. Leonard was seated in a dilapidated armchair reading a magazine devoted to the development of muscles.

Sherm said, "Haven't seen ya around lately, Jimmy boy. Been hidin' from me? Ha. Ha. Ha."

"Been outta town, Sherm. Been to Boston, Detroit, Philly, all over."

"Well, I wanna say I'm glad you're back. And most of all I'm glad you've come to pay up."

"Pay up?" said Jimmy faintly.

"Yeah! Pay up! That's what you come here about, ain't it? And I'm glad for your sake you did. Never liked a deadbeat, eh Leonard?"

The heavyweight assured him that he did not.

Jimmy contemplated the matter.

"Well, I wish I *could* pay up, Sherm," he said at length, then added quickly with what seemed to be an effort at boyish enthusiasm, "and I think I *can*. In a few days, that is. You see, Sherm, I got this Christmas check coming in. Five hundred. At least that's what the folks usually make it — five," and at this point Jimmy held up five uncertain fingers.

"But," he went on, "I haven't got it. *Yet,* that is. You know how things are with the post office these days. All loused up. But who knows? Maybe it's in the box right now! Anyway, Sherm, what I was wondering is if you could keep me supplied for the next few days. Not *much,* Sherm. I don't mean a whole lot. Just eight, ten fixes. Just enough to keep

23

me till that check comes in. Then I'll pay you off and still be able to buy some more besides."

The storekeeper looked down at the top of his desk for a few moments. He continued to look cordial. There was a smile about his lips. But his response, when it came, was to spread his hands and say: "No soap, Jimmy."

"No?" said the young man nervously, unsure of how to handle the refusal he had not really expected.

"No's what I said, and no's what I mean. Sorry, pal, but I can't do it."

"But why, Sherm? Why? I mean, it's not *much*."

The storekeeper cocked his head to one side, but said nothing.

"Besides, I always thought that I was one of your best customers," the young man continued, deciding that a little indignation might help at this point. "Why, the *business* I've sent you!"

"You *were*, Jimmy," Sherm agreed. "You *were* one of my best customers. "But," he said looking directly at the young man, his smile suddenly gone, "you ain't now!"

"I told you I've been away."

"That's a lie, Jimmy. You ain't been away. I know that. Whaddya take me for, anyway? Some kinda chump? I know you've been buyin' off the streets. And I tell ya, it's a risky business, Jimmy. Those guys'll sell you anything and call it smack. It's sure death. They pick stiffs off the street every morning with the needles stuck right in their arm. But if that's the way you wanna go, that's your business. What's worryin' me right now is that you're into me for better than three hundred. Three hundred dollars, Jimmy! And this from a guy who hardly never gives credit. And when I do, it's never for more than fifty or so. But from you? Three hundred. *Three hundred,* buddy! And that's a lot of the old do-re-mi, hey Leonard?"

"Yeah," said the heavyweight without lifting his eyes from the magazine. "A lot."

"I'll pay up. You know that, Sherm," said the young man.

"Oh, I know you'll pay up, all right. My bill collector here will see to that. I'm just sayin' that you ain't one of my best customers no more."

"Look, Sherm," said the young man, and he stooped himself slightly into the posture of beggary, holding out one hand in supplication, "you know where I am in all this. You know I'm hooked bad. You know it's Christmas coming up tomorrow. And where do I get a fix on Christmas when all of you guys are home singing Noel to your kids? Where does it leave me, Sherm? I mean, *where does it LEAVE me?* . . . Do you want to know, Sherm? Do you want to know where it leaves me? Well, I'll tell you! I'll tell you where it leaves me! It leaves me in Bellevue! *Bellevue,* Sherm! Think of it! Bellevue for Christmas! Joy to the world, eh Sherm? Cold turkey for Christmas, Sherm! So look! I'm just asking you this one time! Just enough to tide me over! Just enough for merry Christmas! C'mon, Sherm! Give me a break!"

The previous cordial smile reappeared on Sherm's face.

"Jim!" he pleaded. *"Jim*-boy! Look, pal. Don't talk to me like that. It gets me right here," and Sherm patted his stomach. He spoke genially, but there was steel in his voice too. "I've always been above board with ya, kid. And ya know I didn't give ya the habit. That ya got all by yourself. But I've always given ya good value after ya got it. And I risked

25

my own neck doin' it. Look, kid! I even give ya credit. And rule number one in this business is no credit. Know what I mean when I say no credit? I mean cash! Cash on the barrel head! Don't trust no mainliner! All of us in the business knows that! So why come in here and make with the beggin'?"

"It's not much, Sherm. You're a rich man!"

"Yeah, sure. I'm a rich man. Sittin' here in my mansion and my Brooks Brothers suit. I'm real rich!"

"Just this once."

"Nope."

"Please, Sherm!"

"Don't make me mad, Jimmy. I always liked ya, kid. And I always been good to ya. Three hundred dollars good." Having said as much, Sherm contemplated his goodness a moment before continuing. "Look," he said, adding the timbres of hope to his voice. "Tell ya what! I'm gonna be right here to four-thirty. Why dontcha go out and round up a hundred bucks? With all that dough comin' in, it oughta be a cinch! Bring the hundred to me and we'll put fifty or so on account. Then I'll give ya enough first class smack to keep you noddin' till New Year's."

"But wh—, wh—, where? *Where*, Sherm?" said Jimmy in bewilderment. "Where am I gonna get a hundred bucks?"

Sherm gave the young man a close look, then tilted forward toward the desk.

"That's your problem, kid. Beg. Borrow. Steal. I don't care. All I care is that now I got a lotta work to do. Leonard'll see ya out."

The heavyweight arose, still bowed over his magazine.

"Don't bother," said the young man. "I'm going."

26

Sherm picked up a pencil and began to check a column of figures.

"And don't forget the three hundred, Jimmy," he murmured as the young man brushed aside the curtain and passed through. "Because *I'm* not," he added in a slightly louder voice.

There was no response. Only quick footsteps, the ting-a-ling of the bell, and the slamming of the outside door.

Once up on the street, Jimmy felt a surge of bitterness over Sherm's rejection of what he regarded to be a most reasonable request. By Jimmy's estimate Sherm somehow owed him this small favor, and he hated him for refusing it. He considered turning Sherm in to the police and glanced about for a call box, but none was in sight.

Then, just as abruptly, his anger melted. It was replaced by his more customary feelings of self-pity. As his addiction had deepened, Jimmy, without being aware of it, had begun to feel almost continuously sorry for himself. Why, he would frequently ask himself, did everyone mistreat *him* so? Why did *he* always have the bad luck? Why couldn't some small fragment of good fortune come *his* way?

He turned his back on Sherm's store and began retracing his footsteps to Sheridan Square. A cold winter rain was falling. It matted down his blond, unkempt hair and ran in trickles down the back of his neck, causing him to shudder every now and again.

He was a slightly built young man to begin with, and the lack of nourishment over the past year had given him a rather gaunt look. His clothes were almost as pathetic. The jacket he wore was a threadbare affair. Two pieces of paper would have done as well. It hung from his shoulders as though from a wire coathanger, and from the rear Jimmy's shoulder blades could be seen jutting out like the stumps of wings.

As he walked along, Jimmy put on his traveling face. It was a look which aimed at innocence, but instead registered a curiously recognizable anonymity. For all his indistinctiveness, Jimmy was still something of a type. He belonged to a peculiar breed of city dweller, a kind of subgrouping of the lost, which exists in the center of cities everywhere. Its members are not obvious in the way that certain deviants and derelicts are. Quite the opposite. The Jimmies of this world tend to be on the invisible side. They seem more a part of the city's shadows than anything else. But still almost everyone has had some experience of them. They are the kind who always seem to be walking away from one, or whose murmurs one hears in the dark doorways of side streets, or whom one catches glimpses of at night in a wash of blue fluorescence wolfing hamburgers in stand-up joints.

The ateliers of lampmakers and leatherworkers and antique dealers along 11th Street were aglow with a light and warmth which invited Christmas shoppers inside. But there would be no welcome, Jimmy knew, for such as he. No shopkeeper would be glad to see *him*. It would be perceived at once that Jimmy lived on dreams of one sort or another, dreams from which no profit could be derived. More than once Jimmy had been driven from such shops by lashes of humiliation. The result was that he no longer bothered to enter them.

By the time Jimmy reached Sheridan Square, he had grown quite hungry. He considered heading for a Gospel mission, where he could get both food which he wanted and religion which he did not, but was dissuaded by a more furious hunger than the ordinary one. What he really needed was heroin, and he needed some soon.

By chance he happened to see a former friend standing just out of the reach of the rain while looking through the window of a used bookstore. Jimmy stopped and observed this person from the rear for a few moments. All the while he was thinking of ways in which a loan could be wheedled out of him.

CENTRAL PARK EAST

Shortly after four-thirty on the afternoon of that same Christmas Eve a well-to-do and somewhat aging widow by the name of Helen Pierson Lockroy was standing by the window of her apartment taking a last look at the city before closing the drapes.

The darkness outside had an opaque quality to it. It was not the adamantine darkness of night. It was rather the lingering near-darkness of an overcast winter day's quitting time.

From her point of observation, the 20th floor of a Fifth Avenue apartment house, the leafless trees of Central Park seemed fragile puffs of earth-colored smoke expanded and motionless in midair. Enclosing the park, like a diamond necklace against a swath of dark gray velvet, glistened the lights of Manhattan.

From the particular strand which lay at her feet rose the characteristic sounds of Fifth Avenue traffic — the accelerating roars of bus diesels, the impatient blasts of taxi horns, the whistles of doormen and, far off in the direction of Harlem, the faint, mournful howls of a pack of sirens.

Mrs. Lockroy never seemed to tire of this particular scene at close of day, and especially at this time of year when the weather was wet and alien and people were hurrying to be home. It stirred within her a vague childhood memory, an intimation she'd once had, she couldn't remem-

31

ber where or when, that beneath the pulsations and spasms which attended life there lay, like a bottomless sea, some immeasurably great and serene reality. She'd forgotten the circumstances which called forth this curious idea. Indeed, the intimation itself had grown increasingly blurred as the years had gone by. Nor did it return to her often these days. And when it did, it arrived unexpectedly and departed abruptly, rather like a tanager darting through a thicket of dead wood. For all this, the memory of it was most poignant, a fact which caused her to think that, for all its formlessness, the intimation lay very close to the heart of the final truth of things, whatever that might be.

Since the death of her husband Mrs. Lockroy had pondered the riddle of it more than ever before. She assumed that its explanation also lay cradled somewhere in her memory, and she would fain lay hold on that explanation. Yet it remained obscured, entangled in the welter of the far more mundane recollections that crowded her mind.

Still, at certain times the meaning of that intimation seemed more accessible to her than at others; and never more so than at dusk with all of its bittersweet invitations to remembrance: day's end, toil's end, homegoing, the mystery of families and food, the pillow beneath one's head, the rehearsal for death, the skein of dreams, the promise of rebirth. So on this night she once more awaited the revelation. But when after 15 minutes it failed to come, she pulled the drawstring.

The drapes hastened together.

The room to which she turned was about what one might expect for someone of her years and means. It was spacious, it was overheated, it bore a lingering odor of cold cream.

The hand of a decorator could be seen in the various muted whites which dominated the room's decor — white drapes of raw silk, white wool rug, shiny white upholstery on the antiqued white finish of period furniture. There were white shades on lamps, white cushions scattered over a white sofa, and wallpaper of woven grass bleached white. Everything white. Widow white. A whiteness which a man would find oppressive, but which suited a lonely old lady of 76 quite perfectly.

Mrs. Lockroy sat down on her favorite hard chair and, as tended to be her custom at this time of the day, began a conversation with her husband.

"I suppose you know by now," she told him in a resigned voice, "that I'll be alone for Christmas."

"Alone?" He sounded somewhat detached, sitting there in his armchair. It was the tone he adopted when he would rather be reading the paper than talking. "I thought you'd made plans for Isabelle Schuyler to be here."

"I did. But she's not coming."

"Why?"

"Her maid called yesterday to say she'd taken sick."

"Sick, eh? What's wrong with her this time?" he asked without the least trace of sympathy.

"She didn't say."

"Hmmmmph!" said Mr. Lockroy skeptically.

He'd always been impatient with vague explanations, didn't believe most of them, at best regarded them as evasions of the truth. He had a look which accompanied this particular displeasure — a raising of the eyebrows, a flaring of the nostrils, a pursing of the lips — the which, taken together, as much as said, "A likely story!"

She only wished she could see it. That was the part which bothered her about these conversations. She could *hear* him all right. There was no mistaking that flat midwestern voice of his. It was as real to her as the ticking of the French clock on the escritoire. But the face eluded her, refused to come into focus despite her repeated hints that he materialize then and there in that armchair where for so many years he'd sat and read the newspaper before dinner. He would not do so, however. And it was quite maddening, especially when she found herself compelled to break off the conversation and step into the bedroom, where his picture rested on the bureau, just to remind herself of what sort of person she was talking to.

"Well, whatever her reasons, she won't be coming here . . ." said Mrs. Lockroy, punctuating the sentence with a huge sigh. "I must tell you in all frankness, Elwood," she continued, "that I don't much care for the idea of being alone on Christmas."

"No one likes to be alone on Christmas," he observed.

"It will be the first time, you know. I've never spent a Christmas alone in my entire life."

He seemed to put the newspaper down and look at her for the first time since the conversation began.

"I guess things have been pretty tough for you since I left."

An element of compassion in his words touched a raw nerve which, in turn, produced a quaver in her voice.

"You'll never know," she answered, trying her best to even it out.

His response, whenever she grew emotional, was to become sensible, practical.

"Why don't you just call around and see if there's some-one who would put up with you?"

She warded off the suggestion with her hands.

"Oh Elwood, I couldn't!"

"You wouldn't have to come right out and ask. You could just tell them you were calling to wish a merry Christmas and, in the course of things, say that you'd planned to have Isabelle here and she got sick and couldn't come."

"And hope they'd take the hint?"

"Of course."

She shook her head at this display of naiveté. Men, she reminded herself, were rather on the coarse side when it came to the nuances of social give and take.

"They'd see through it in a minute, Elwood. Then they'd feel sorry for me, and you know how I despise pity."

He seemed to shrug and return his attention to the paper, with a resulting lull in the conversation.

It reminded her of another conversation, which had taken place several weeks before. She'd been talking to Elwood about all sorts of matters when she heard a noise in the next room. When she went to investigate, she discovered that the day maid had stayed a little later than usual and was, at that moment, running a dust rag over the highboy. Quite obviously she had heard the entire conversation — or at least Mrs. Lockroy's end of it.

Helen Lockroy couldn't avoid the stricken look on the girl's face. Nevertheless, both of them acted as if nothing unusual had taken place and chatted for 10 minutes on various cleaning matters.

Tonight, however, she heard no sounds from either the next room or any of the other eight in her apartment.

"I don't mind being alone most of the time," she said, attempting to nurse the conversation along. "You know that."

"Yes," he said simply.

"But Christmas brings such memories. I find it hard to be alone just now . . ." She paused, then said, "Elwood?"

"Hmmmm?"

"Do you remember when we were first married and lived in Forest Hills in that tiny apartment?"

He seemed to nod.

"Do you remember how small that parlor was, and how the first year you came home with a huge tree which took up at least half of it? Why, we practically had to *chop* our way into the kitchen."

"Those were happy times for us," he murmured.

"And then the cat—what was his name?"

"Phillip."

"Phillip climbed to the top of the tree, and the whole thing, ornaments and all, fell over."

"That cat's probably still running," he chuckled.

"We laughed until the tears ran down."

"You did, in any event."

"And so did you, Elwood. It won't do you a bit of good to deny it."

"We had a good life together, Helen. I was a lucky man."

"Oh Elwood, I love to think of all those Christmases we had together, and yet at the same time I can hardly bear it, I tremble so. It's not fair that life should come to this. That when we've finally learned to treasure life, and filled it with good things, it should just be snatched away from us and leave us to be buried in some junkyard. Because that's what they are, Elwood. Junkyards. However well the grass is kept,

36

however often they straighten the monuments and rub out the naughty words, they're junkyards still. I tell you, Elwood, if I'd been God, I would have arranged it differently."

"Helen."

"Yes?"

She said it faintly, for when he spoke her name a certain way, it signaled that something momentous was about to follow. She had an inkling of what it might be, and dreaded to hear it.

"Why don't you call Vivian?" he asked simply.

"Vivian?"

"I seem to remember that was the name we gave her."

"I . . . I can't, Elwood. You know that."

"But of course you can," he said impatiently. "All you have to do is pick up the telephone and dial a few numbers."

She shook her head. It was as much a gesture of resignation as refusal.

"We've been through this so many times before, Elwood," she complained. "I don't see why you insist on bringing it up again."

"She's your daughter, Helen. *Our* daughter. The only child we have."

"Don't you mean the only child we *had?* I'm not sure I care to look on her as my daughter anymore. Not after what happened."

"It's all in the past now."

"Not for me it isn't. I feel it as keenly now as when it happened. And when I think of all we did for her!"

"Now Helen, be sensible. We can't be sure *what* we did for her, or failed to do. There's too much of the unknown in raising children to go about assigning blame. As for the rest, she's only human after all. Everyone makes mistakes."

"Not mistakes like that, Elwood! It was a deliberate act if I ever saw one: So calculated. So cruel. That's the part I can't forget. It was as if she set out to destroy us, Elwood. You know it and I know it. And she did a good job of it, as everyone agrees. Even so," Helen Lockroy added bitterly, "I might have forgiven her for all that if . . ."

"I know what you're going to say, Helen, and I beg you not to."

"Why shouldn't I? Everyone else says it. Everyone else knows that she sent you to your grave."

"Well, you've said it!" he exclaimed in disgust.

"And when that happened, it was all over for me."

"You can't be sure she sent me to my grave."

"Even the doctor said so."

"Well, if he did, he had no right to," was the irritated reply. "Doctors don't know all that much, no matter what they think. Besides, for all you know he might have been covering up his own mistakes. Those injections he was giving really didn't agree with me. I felt dizzy most of those last few months."

"I know that. But he said it was an emotional reaction that capped it off. And when I asked if he were referring to Vivian's doings, he said I could draw my own conclusions."

"My conclusion would be to get a new doctor. As for Vivian, don't you think the possibility crossed her mind too?"

"What do you mean?"

"Don't you suppose she's spent the past eight years accusing herself of my death? And if she has, don't you think that's punishment enough?"

"She didn't even come to your funeral," said Mrs. Lockroy, disregarding the question.

"Oh well, I didn't mind. There could have been any number of reasons why she didn't make it."

"Do you really think so?" said Helen Lockroy, giving a sarcastic edge to her voice.

"Oh, I don't know. All I'm saying is why not let the past go? You should be talking to Vivian these days, not me. So why not make another go at it? You know where she is. You know that she's probably all alone too. And awfully broke. And much too proud to ask for anything. It's been tough for her, Helen, picking up the pieces. But she's done all right. She's held down the same job for better than five years now, and paid back nearly everything. You've got to give her credit for that. So why not go ahead and make that call?"

"I can't."

"It's Christmas Eve, Helen. It's the time to be giving things."

"And what do you suggest I give her? A gun, so she could finish things off by shooting me?"

"For heaven's sake, Helen! You don't have to get *dramatic* about it! Just give her your forgiveness. That's simple enough. And it won't cost you a dime, either. Just tell her that everything is all right now and you're ready to make a new start."

"I'm not a forgiving person, Elwood. I find it hard to forgive even myself for my various shortcomings."

He pondered her words a few moments before answering.

"Perhaps that's where the trouble lies, Helen," he said at last. "Perhaps you're too hard on yourself."

"What do you mean by that?"

"Only that a person who can't forgive himself isn't likely to forgive someone else."

"You're talking plain gibberish, Elwood!"

"Oh, I don't know. If someone makes allowances for himself, if he's good to himself, I rather imagine he'll spread it around a little."

"Well, it sounds like so much selfishness to me," she sniffed.

"There's not that much difference between selfishness and generosity. One's a stillborn version of the other, that's all."

"You're not making sense, Elwood. You're just saying words. And what they boil down to, I suppose, is the fact that you think I'm stingy."

"Oh, not in the miserly sense."

"I should say not," she declared loftily. "I'm a soft touch for every charity that comes my way. And there are quite a few these days, Elwood. I can't open my mail without having some half-starved child peep out at me."

"Still, I wouldn't exactly call you a soft touch. You always gave those charities a pretty close look before you sent them anything."

"I was taught to be careful," was her prim reply.

"Well, all I'm saying is that it's a bit difficult to be careful and generous at the same time, just like it's hard to be careful and forgiving at the same time."

Mrs. Lockroy set her chin.

"I don't want to hear any more on this subject, I think,"

she told him. "You kept preaching about it when you were alive. And now that you're dead, you still keep harping on it."

"What else am I supposed to do with my harp?"

"I would suggest you play it," she said crossly.

"That still leaves us with the question of Christmas. What are you going to do about that?"

"I don't know. I haven't made up my mind. Stay here by myself, I suppose. Watch the television. Go to bed."

"The least you could do is get yourself dressed up and go out to dinner," he admonished her.

"Ha! And be seen eating alone on Christmas Eve? Never! I'll be perfectly content to take a few things out of the ice box."

"All of which brings me to say that you're not eating right these days."

It was true. There was no denying it. Her meals lately had become little more than a picking at leftovers. Even worse, she was eating too many sweets these days. Indeed, she would gladly subsist entirely on Danish buns and cookies, ice cream and heavily sugared coffee, if it weren't for that thin-lipped autocrat within who included nutritional matters among his various concerns. Still, her conscience wasn't forceful enough to persuade her to prepare a decent meal for herself.

"I know that," she admitted. "But it's hard cooking for just one person."

He seemed to be shaking his head and clicking his tongue now. "Really, you shouldn't be alone like this."

"You don't know how lonely I am."

"Your friends . . ."

"It's not the same, Elwood. I feel lonely even when I'm

41

with them, which isn't often these days. I just don't have the energy to keep up friendships the way I used to. Besides, they keep *dying* on me. I can't tell you how much I've paid the florist this past year alone. Really, it's all so unsettling I just keep to myself. Sometimes I get the odd feeling that even *I* don't exist anymore. I feel that *you're* the one who's alive and *I'm* the one who's dead. . . . And I must say, I felt it strongly today when the mail came."

"Something you read in a letter?"

"Oh no. Nothing like that. It wasn't what *came* in the mail. It's what *didn't* come that made me feel that way. You see, it was the last delivery before Christmas. And as I was looking through the notices of January white sales, I realized all at once that I hadn't gotten so much as a single gift for Christmas."

"No gift for Christmas?" He seemed quite astonished.

"Nothing," she said in a tiny voice, trying to sound indifferent about it all, but sighing nevertheless. "Nothing at all. No benefit fruitcake. No box of candy from the drugstore. No sachet. No bath oil. No embroidered handkerchiefs. No feather flowers. Nothing. Nothing, nothing, nothing."

"Why, that's dreadful, Helen! Why didn't you tell me right away?"

"What difference would *that* have made? *You're* not going to give me anything; that's for sure."

"Maybe so," he agreed. "But I might have worked something out. At the very least I'd have had you call the post office. I imagine your packages got lost in the rush."

"I wouldn't be too sure of it, Elwood. You haven't noticed it, but I've been getting less and less since you left me. . . . Oh, it's partly my fault, I'll be frank to admit. After all, guess who it was who told her friends that since we had everything we needed now, we should agree not to give each other anything for Christmas? Well, we stopped, all right. And all that came of it is that when Christmas rolls around we all feel sorry for ourselves."

"Is it the first time?"

"The first time what?"

"The first time you've never received a single present for Christmas?"

"So far as I can remember," she said, and shrugged her shoulders to show that she was really quite indifferent to it all.

"It's not right, Helen! *Everyone* should get at least some little thing for Christmas!"

"Well, I think so too. But what can I do? I can't go out and buy something for myself."

"It's an idea."

"A ridiculous idea! From a ridiculous old woman that's lived too long."

"Nonsense! No one lives too long. Take it from me."

"No, take it from *me*, Elwood. When you reach the point where you're no use to anyone, when you find you don't count for anything and are just taking up space and no one cares whether you live or die, then you're better off dead."

"Feeling sorry for yourself won't solve anything," he observed.

"How else am I supposed to feel all alone on Christmas Eve?"

"Don't feel anything. Just . . . just be *good* to yourself."

His voice had grown a trifle thin, a factor of which she now took notice.

"You're not going so soon!" she said.

"I suppose I must. I've stayed too long already."

"Please, Elwood! Don't go yet!" she pleaded.

"You know I don't have any say about that. But I promise something!"

"Promise what?"

"I promise that when I get to the place where I'm being kept these days, I shall beg a gift for you."

His voice had grown so faint she could hardly hear him.

"A gift, Elwood? Whatever do you mean? What kind of gift could be sent from over there?"

"Something you'd least expect, I imagine. That's the way they usually work things."

"I can't hear you very well."

". . . a surprise . . ." said a wraithlike voice.

"Whatever are you talking about, Elwood? What kind of gift do you mean? Anyway, whatever it is, I don't want it. All I want is for you to stay with me awhile longer," she said, and held out one arm toward the shadows. But his chair was empty. He was gone now. She knew it, resigned herself to it, and told herself there was nothing else to do but go out into the kitchen and prepare a bit of supper.

She turned on the burner under the kettle, arranged a salad plate and silverware for herself on the kitchen table, then rummaged about in the refrigerator for something to take the edge off her hunger.

An odd silence lurked this night among the white cabinets. The kitchen in her apartment was located toward the rear of the building, away from the street, away from the city noises which penetrated into the other rooms. It lay in a kind of acoustical isolation, with the result that all she now heard was the rasp of the fire's tongue along the kettle's bottom.

The sound comforted her. But silence still lingered menacingly in various enameled corners with the threat that once more it would emerge and weave a spell about her. Involutional depression, her doctor called these spells. What they amounted to were days of lassitude and random sadness, of mild self-loathing and grating doubt, of emptiness at the marrow.

She fully anticipated such a depression on this night. But five minutes later she found herself turning edgy instead. Something had angered her; she didn't know what. The anger was deep and unidentifiable. It surfaced as an irritability as fretful and feverish as the sunburst of tiny blue jets underneath the kettle.

And just why *should* the water take so long to boil? *That* was the question which bothered her at the moment! To her way of thinking, it had certainly never taken this long before.

All the fault, she assumed, of the utility company, which doubtless was turning out an inferior grade of gas these days. Yes, and likely charging more for it in the bargain!

When at last she began to eat, she did so with angry little nibbles. Her coffee she sipped as though it were gall. And when it came time to put away the supper things, she clattered the dishes unmercifully and slammed the refrigerator door.

Afterwards, when she had retreated to the living room, she repented somewhat and decided it might be wise to uncover the reason for this eruption of anger, a reason which,

she believed, functioned rather on the order of a wall switch that could be turned off if one could but find it.

Curiously, she found it. To her mortification, the cause of her anger turned out to be nothing more consequential than the aforementioned lack of a gift to open on Christmas Day. That was all there was to it.

There followed the obligation to hector herself a little. Wasn't this, she scolded, a ridiculous reason to fret? Wasn't it behaving just like a spoiled child?

"Shame on you!" Mrs. Lockroy said aloud.

Still, she concluded after further consideration, better to feel angry than sorry for oneself! Better pique than self-pity! And furthermore, now that she thought about it, didn't she have some small *right* to feel put out? Wasn't her anger, at least in some measure, justified? Was it so strange, after all, to feel aggravated and out of sorts after being treated so shabbily on Christmas Eve?

"Most assuredly not!" she announced to the walls of her apartment.

Hers, she now discovered, was an eminently normal reaction to a most provoking set of circumstances. It was nothing more than what one might expect, given the conditions. After all, who *wouldn't* feel peevish at being utterly forgotten on Christmas Eve? Who *wouldn't* be annoyed over such outrageous neglect? Indeed, if ever in the history of the world there was a justifiable grievance, hers was it! As for slamming the refrigerator door, that too was a perfectly understandable reaction!

Discovering that this line of thinking brought with it a measure of relief, she continued. And wasn't it just like people these days, treating the elderly so? Just shoving them

47

off into corners and forgetting them on holidays and leaving them to die alone! It wasn't right. It simply was not right! It wasn't fair that, on a night when millions of people the world over were whetting their appetite for the opening of gifts, a few old people like herself were getting nothing at all. The indignity of it! Why, even the Chinese, communists though they were, did better by their old folks than *that!*

As the righteous displeasure of Mrs. Lockroy began to crest, a stray idea, like an impish beam of light, came along and suggested the logical solution to her difficulties. There was nothing particularly novel about that suggestion. Indeed she had touched on the possibility herself earlier in the evening and then quite sensibly rejected it.

The solution was this: Since no one else seemed disposed to give her a Christmas gift, there always remained the option of buying one for herself. After all, she exclaimed to herself, if one doesn't look out for number one, who will? If others remain unconcerned about a person's welfare, then what alternatives are there but to see to them oneself?

In this manner Mrs. Lockroy soon became overcome with what can only be described as an errant bit of nonsense. What earlier that evening she had dismissed with ridicule now began to seem plausible. Not only plausible but quite axiomatic as well. Indeed, the belief that people who weren't given gifts for Christmas were under a moral obligation to buy the same for themselves began to take on in her mind the characteristics of one of those self-evident and inexorable principles on which the very well-being of the universe depends, a principle somewhat akin to the law of gravity.

The moment all this became clear the anger vanished,

to be replaced by a spirit of determination. Since it had come to this, she told herself, she would *have* her Christmas gift! And it would be a proper gift too! No dime store item for *her*. No piece of bric-a-brac that got thrown out before New Year's. No indeed! If she, Helen Pierson Lockroy, was reduced to the ignominy of having to provide her own Christmas present, then it would have to be something — well, nice. Something different. Something exquisite. Something she'd always wanted but been too timid to buy. It would have to be expensive, of course. Extravagant, even. It might not even be amiss to dip into capital for the right sort of gift. . . .

The truth of it was that Mrs. Lockroy already knew precisely what she had in mind. Earlier that week she had seen a picture of it in the pages of a magazine devoted to the interests of people who dwelt in the environs of New York City. It had been a black and white photograph of a necklace being offered for sale by the most prestigious jeweler on Fifth Avenue. The text below had been written with characteristic understatement. Merely a sparse description of the necklace, the number of carats involved, and its price written out in words instead of numbers.

At the time Mrs. Lockroy had been intrigued by the necklace, though shocked at its price. *She,* she advised herself, would never pay *that* for *this!* Or was it *this* for *that?* No matter. Whichever, she, Helen Pierson Lockroy, would simply *never* lay out such a sum of money for a bauble that had no other purpose than personal adornment.

But still, she told herself, as she examined the photograph, it *did* look rather elegant. That glittering rope of diamonds! It would go splendidly with that white evening gown of hers that had been packed away in mothballs for

49

better than 20 years now. And that emerald! Why, it looked like it had been plucked from the eyesocket of a pagan idol! She'd never *seen* such a splendid gem, and couldn't help wondering how it would feel suspended from her neck.

So it was that she had mused from time to time during the past few days on the question of who in the world would want to own such an extravagant piece of jewelry.

Now, on this Christmas Eve, the answer had come. To put it quite simply, *she* did! She, Helen Pierson Lockroy, wanted that necklace! And not only that, she meant to have it! It now became her firm intention to buy it without further delay. She would make it her Christmas gift to herself. That diamond and emerald affair would become the gift that no one had given her.

Having arrived at this resolve, Mrs. Lockroy glanced at the clock on the escritoire.

Five forty-five.

There was still time.

THE FIRST SHOP

Having left 42nd Street behind, Rosie continued on down Fifth Avenue. He found, however, that along this section of the avenue stores were fewer and more specialized. One store sold nothing but fire extinguishing equipment. Another dealt in various kinds of uniforms. A third concerned itself with the distribution of kitchen equipment to hotels and restaurants.

When at last Rosie came upon a store window which offered nothing more to the viewer than a display of floor scrubbing machines with large red bows on the handles, it occurred to him that the time had come to cross the street and head back up Fifth Avenue on the other side.

A few score steps brought him to a corner crosswalk. At the same time it brought him into the vicinity of a rather narrow, isolated store which seemed to compensate for its size and insignificance with an interior ablaze with furious white light. From where he stood, Rosie could see hanging across the upper section of one of the plate glass windows a banner on which had been printed in large block letters:

GIGANTIC CLOSEOUT SALE!

Its counterpart on the other side carried the words:

BARGAINS GALORE!

Scattered around these two signs were a host of lesser auxiliaries with various other urgent messages: SACRIFICE!

LOST OUR LEASE! BELOW COST! EVERYTHING MUST GO! OUR LOSS IS YOUR GAIN! BUY! BUY! BUY!

Rosie, whose experiences in Harlem had taught him to be somewhat wary of human promises, drifted uncertainly in the direction of the store window to see what this assault upon the eyes might be all about. What he found, as anyone who has ever trod the streets of an American metropolis already realizes, was a display of the gadgetry and gimcracks, the knickknacks and trinkets by which tourists are persuaded to memorialize their visits.

The first thing on the other side of the store window to catch Rosie's eye was a number of bronzed souvenir replicas of the Empire State Building lined up like a squad of soldiers. These were flanked on one side by a dozen or so wooden plaques, stained a dark mahogany in color, from each of which protruded a pair of chromium-plated hands loosely clasped in prayer. On the other side were rows of china salt and pepper shakers in the form of grinning little boys and girls with openings like broken-off teeth for the salt and pepper to come through.

To the rear of these items were exhibited various other consequences of losing one's lease. Spread out on ascending risers were bud vases and miniature portable radios, opera glasses and electric pants creasers, whiskey glasses with faces painted on them, and aqua-blue ash trays flecked with gold. Draped across the partition to the rear was an arrangement of women's kerchiefs with a silver sheen in the center upon which a somewhat distorted sketch of the George Washington Bridge had been superimposed, and a swirling combination of electric reds and greens around the border.

As Rosie's eyes moved over these treasures one by one,

they were suddenly attracted by something which could scarcely escape one's attention. It was a mirror — a hand mirror of the type which calls up pictures of milady seated in her boudoir holding up such a mirror with one dainty hand while the other is poised over the back of an impeccable coiffure.

There was certainly no shortage of these mirrors. Around the principal display item lay a fan-shaped arrangement of many others. And behind these an additional stack in white pasteboard boxes.

The fact that so many of them remained yet unsold on Christmas Eve did not dim the immediate attraction Rosie felt for them. To his young and uncritical eyes they were objects of breathtaking beauty. What made them more wonderful still was the placard beside them which proclaimed the astonishing information that the price of these marvelous hand mirrors was merely $1.97.

No sooner had this inconceivability registered itself upon Rosie's mind than he realized that at last he had found his mother's Christmas gift. After all, he reasoned with himself, what could be more appropriate for someone so beautiful as his mother than this handsome mirror?

If there remained any lingering doubts in his mind, they were quickly dissipated by a brief reverie. In his imagination Rosie projected himself forward in time to the next morning. He pictured his mother opening her Christmas gift. With the unclouded vision of the young he could see her removing the mirror from its box. Without any difficulty whatever he could discern the look of surprise which came over her face, a look which soon became transformed into one of unalloyed delight. Her expression told him all he wanted to know. The mirror, beyond any question, was the most lovely gift she had ever received.

The fantasy expanded somewhat, and gradually grew all out of proportion, as these things tend to do. Before long Rosie's imagination created a situation in which the mirror had become his mother's favorite possession. He dreamt that it came to be assigned a place of special honor, far from the hands of marauding little sisters. He envisioned a time in which it was removed from its place only on special occasions when it could be reverently displayed to favored guests. He could almost hear the ooohs and ahhhs of admiration, almost perceive the looks of envy from people whose sons had never gotten *them* anything so wonderful.

Before very long Rosie's reverie had become so palpable that it very nearly lifted him by the seat of his trousers and propelled him into the store.

The only person inside was the clerk, a rather slovenly adolescent female dressed in a blue smock. At the moment Rosie entered she was standing by the cash register eating a doughnut. The white paper bag from which it had been taken rested beside her on the counter.

Rosie did not hesitate in making his wants known.

"Kin I see the mirra?" he asked.

"Right behinja," replied the girl without bothering to look at him. For some reason she seemed obliged to keep her eyes on the street outside. Whatever the reason, whether boredom or curiosity or some irrepressible desire to be set at liberty, her eyes — an opaque blue under brows which passed one another in the center, focused on the street outside and seemed incapable of being fixed upon any more immediate surroundings.

At her words Rosie turned and saw a shelf piled high with pasteboard boxes like those in the window. On top rested a sample mirror.

Fingers trembling with excitement, Rosie reached for it. He took the precious object into his hands.

The mirror was much lighter than he anticipated. There was a massive look to it, but actually it weighed very little. Its plastic handle was a robin's egg blue in color. It had been made to resemble a Persian column, with fluting running along the shaft and ornate cornices at either end. Beneath the lower cornice the handle petered out into an elaborate, lozenge-shaped appendage. The upper end, however, flowed outward and became the backing of the mirror. The backing, like the mirror itself, was oval in shape and an unambiguous pink in hue. Upon its center had been superimposed a cameolike impression of a cupid. To augment the overall impression, the edges had been melted and formed into a white doily which managed to give the outline of the mirror a ruffled look.

Rosie inspected the back of the mirror closely, marveling at the ability of ordinary mortals to fabricate such an elegant device. He concluded his inspection by turning the mirror over and examining the pleased expression on a face which had a familiar look to it.

"That's real nice," he said aloud, expecting immediate confirmation from the salesgirl.

"Yeah . . . If ya like Frenchy things," murmured the girl through a mouthful of doughnut. Her eyes were still fixed on the street outside. She chewed the doughnut in a slow, dreamy cadence.

"My mom sure do," volunteered Rosie.

"Then whyn't ya buy it for her?" said the girl absently.

"Yeah. I am."

"Just bring me one over here then," said the girl.

Rosie took one of the pasteboard boxes and laid it on the counter.

The girl looked dubiously at it.

"Why dontcha get her one of those radios there?" she suggested. "Just cost ya nine ninety-nine."

"She already got one," was Rosie's not entirely truthful reply.

"Too bad," said the girl thoughtfully. Then she added: "Want it gift wrap?"

"Like how?"

"Do it up in Christmas paper and a nice ribbon."

"Yeah, sure."

At this the girl removed a pair of scissors from her smock. But before beginning to wrap the box, she took one final look at the street.

"Gettin' empty out there," she observed in a sad, somewhat resigned voice. "Sometimes so many people you can't see the other side. First time in six weeks."

The paper for the box came off a large roll. It had a gold cast to it. The girl trimmed the paper to size, then wrapped the box quickly, expertly, indifferently. She fastened the folds with cellophane tape.

"I got to give you a gold ribbon," the salesgirl said. "We usually do a red, but we're out of it, Okay?"

Rosie nodded.

She tied the box with the ribbon four ways. She then snipped off a few extra lengths of ribbon and added them to the knot. Last of all she scraped these ribbon fragments with the sharp edge of her scissors blade. And lo! each of them shriveled up into a pile of tight curls.

"That all?" said the girl when she had finished.

"Yeah," said Rosie a trifle breathlessly, for he had never before seen such an exquisitely wrapped package.

"Now let's see," said the girl after another brief inspection of the street. She reached for a pencil and began to write as she talked.

"That's one ninety-seven for the mirror, plus . . . uh . . . eight cents tax, and twenty-five for the gift wrap — which comes to . . . uh . . . two thirty-seven. No, two thirty-*eight!*"

These calculations had begun by bewildering Rosie. They ended by devastating him.

"But . . . but . . . but I don't have it," he protested. "I mean, I thought the mirra was a dollah ninety-seven."

"You fergot the tax and the gift wrap, sonny."

"I din't know it cost somethin'."

"You think we gift wrap for free?"

"I . . . I . . ." stuttered Rosie.

"Canchew *read,* kid?"

The girl nodded in the direction of a sign behind her which clearly informed customers that gift wrapping involved a surcharge of 25 cents.

"I din't see it. Honest. I ain't got the money. I mean, I gotta keep some for the bus."

The girl looked sternly down at him. However, she couldn't see much. Her view of his face was blocked by the bill of his cap. All she could see were the nub of his nose and the outline of his lips.

Perhaps his lips quivered a bit. Perhaps she imagined it. Perhaps she was just tired. Whatever, the girl relented.

"I should make ya take 'nother one in a plain bag," she said. "But . . . what the heck! It's Christmas Eve. So I'll let it go this one time. But I still gotta charge you some tax. So we'll just make it two dollars even."

Rosie withdrew the compacted dollar bills from his jacket, unfolded them carefully, removed the change, then counted the bills one after the other into the shopgirl's hand. He then picked up his precious, precious gift and walked out onto Fifth Avenue.

And if he seemed to mingle more easily with those outside, it may have been because this transaction had caused him to become, as it were, a colleague of the human race. He was an alien no longer. He was neither a child, nor black, nor poor. Now he was a fellow-last-minute-buyer. Now he was a person who had shared with nearly everyone up and down Fifth Avenue the magnificent experience of getting that last, that most important, that most perfect gift of all in the very nick of time.

It did not occur to Rosie to walk directly crosstown for the Lexington Avenue bus. For him the way back would be the way he came — up Fifth Avenue to 59th Street, then over to Lexington. Rosie, after all, was only 11 years old and not inclined toward efficiency. Besides, there was half of the avenue he had not seen. So at 41st Street he crossed Fifth Avenue in front of the Public Library and began to head uptown on its western side.

By now the temperature had begun to drop. The drizzle had stopped. The air had taken on that sterile, expectant odor which one associates with the near advent of snow. Wind fits pushed at Rosie's jacket and rustled the curled ends of the ribbon on his package.

He passed a bank whose tidy counters and desks and potted plants — not to mention the door to a gigantic vault — were separated from him by nothing more than a large sheet of plate glass. A clock inside informed Rosie that already he was past due at home. Still, however, the package in his hand seemed a talisman against the consequences of any late arrival, so he was not inclined to hurry.

At Rockefeller Center he took a detour to his left and made a perambulatory inspection of the Christmas tree. He then walked over to the ice rink, where he saw a solitary young woman in an abbreviated black costume skating backwards. The runners of her skates made a sound against the ice like a butcher's knife being whetted on steel.

Walking back to the Avenue, Rosie stopped long enough to examine a cutaway model of an airplane interior which was poised in the window of a travel agency. He marveled that such things really existed, that people actually entered them and made themselves comfortable in them and ate dinner in them while flying to the ends of the earth.

Fifth Avenue, when he reached it once more, seemed colder and more deserted than ever. Odd bits of paper had taken to skittering along the streets. The pieces would roll and skip until snared by the post of a streetlamp or firebox, at which point the life would flutter out of them.

A distinct numbness had begun to develop in Rosie's feet and hands and nose. His nose he would hide in the crook of his arm and let the wet warmness of his exhalations thaw it. But for his hands and feet there was no such comfort.

Rosie soon began to wish for a large department store or a stand-up restaurant where he could enter and warm himself without being noticed. But let a person want something so simple as that and he is apt, as in this case, to be presented with block after block of small exclusive shops, none of which could be expected to offer gladly a bit of ordinary free warmth. In any event, most of them were closed.

But then, when he was about to despair of finding such a place, there came to him the sight of a dark building with several pairs of large doors through which people seemed to be passing without hindrance.

Rosie turned aside. He examined the facade of this building. While it looked rather like a medieval fortress, Rosie had no difficulty recognizing before him a church of some sort. The humorless saints who guarded the portals gave it away. That and the insets of stained glass on either side, behind which a dim fire seemed to burn.

For Rosie this edifice was not at all like the storefront church his mother sometimes attended. Still, he reasoned within himself as he stood outside in the cold, churches were *supposed* to be friendly places, or so he had heard various preachers say. And this, Rosie assumed, meant *all* churches, great and small, cathedrals and storefronts. As far as the instance at hand was concerned, surely the semideities who ran this place would not mind sharing a little heat in the back of the church with someone so clearly a human being as a frozen last-minute Christmas shopper!

And so, holding his package before him as a badge of his identity with humanity at large, Rosie mounted the great stone steps of the church and pushed open the door.

Inside it smelled of perfume and furniture oil. The vestibule was neither cold nor warm, but something in between. The genuine article, as far as heat was concerned, seemed to be on the other side of some leaded glass doors.

Rosie hesitated, then pulled the door open and walked into the nave of the church.

He was a bit too cold to be impressed by the church's interior — a 13th-century affair though barely 50 years old. But then, neither was the congregation, for the 100 or so people who had gathered there sat dully in their places wrapped in the introversions of piety and clearly unenthusiastic about such matters as the elaborately carved reredos against the east wall, or the immense spotlighted altar with its eight massive candlesticks, or the bountiful arrangements of evergreens, or the full rich organ sounds which seemed to descend in layers from the dark and vaulted ceiling.

Rosie started down the aisle. As he did so, an incipient difficulty presented itself. A large, rather florid man wearing a white carnation in his lapel and carrying a sheaf of church programs as though they were a hand of oversized rummy cards began to move in on Rosie's line of march. An encounter was inevitable. But, miraculously, this usher was overtaken by another.

"Ohfergodssake, Ed, let the kid siddown," the other man seemed to be saying as Rosie slipped into the second pew from the rear.

The first usher responded with a whisper which contained an unusual amount of sibilants. "Sssssss . . . shhhhhh . . . shhh . . . ss . . . sssss . . . shh . . . sss."

The only word which Rosie heard clearly was "trouble." And at this point it must be admitted that Rosie suffered a momentary disappointment that the package in his hand did not carry the authority he had anticipated.

But in the end he was left alone, and that was all that mattered for the moment. As he sat down, warmth came about him like a soft embrace. It caressed his ears and soothed his neck. It invaded his nostrils and brushed at the glitter in the corner of his eyes.

Once he felt a bit more like his usual self, Rosie began to watch the people as they passed him on their way down the aisle. Nearly everyone turned and gave Rosie a look of mild astonishment. Among these was a sandy-haired young man who seemed as out of place in that church as Rosie himself.

Rosie returned the young man's look. As their glances intersected, Rosie briefly wondered what a man without a necktie might be doing in such a church as this. Simultaneously, the young man was wondering what a black boy who had neglected to remove his cap was doing there.

By the time the service began, a number of people were sitting in the vicinity of Rosie. They, unlike him, possessed service leaflets. And when it came time to sing, they stood on their feet and began to wheeze in dolorous, restrained voices:

Oh come, all ye faithful, Joyful and triumphant,
Oh come ye, oh come ye to Bethlehem . . .

They intoned their dirge in strained, barely audible voices, as if they feared that to really sing out would bring round an usher with the threat of dismissal on his lips.

Afterwards a sacred figure in the front of the church spoke. The congregation kneeled in deference. Then a choir sang. Then there was more speaking. Standing. Singing. Kneeling. Speaking.

Rosie was warm now. He felt that his feet were really his own once more. He was ready to go. He knew he ought to go. But the amplified voice which seemed all around him had taken on a hypnotic quality.

After awhile Rosie's head fell forward, and he slept.

THE SECOND SHOP

Some three hours after leaving Sherm's, Jimmy returned to his lodgings in the East Village. He had a single room there, paid for by the week. It was located in a ramshackle brick apartment building which had lately been subdivided by its owners into a festering warren characterized by the initials SRO — which letters sometimes stand for "Single Room Occupancy" and sometimes for "Standing Room Only," the distinction being somewhat academic in either event.

As Jimmy stepped through the front door, the foyer of the building did its best to greet him with old-time geniality. It enveloped him in its customary winter warmth — a warmth which suggested the odor of scorched paint on radiators. It provided his feet with a firm footing of tiny hexagons of white tile with a curiously gritty feel to them. It offered the same old vista — the window on the right through which the light of the sun never passed directly but only its reflection off drab walls, the postal boxes on the left whose tiny brass doors had long ago been pried open and left to hang crazily from bent hinges, the stairway directly ahead with its ornate iron risers.

Jimmy's room was located on the third floor.

He made his ascent up the ill-lighted stairway, then walked back along a narrow hallway past a series of varnished doors until he came to his own.

The door was, as usual, unlocked.

He walked in and closed the door behind him. With a motion grown habitual through repetition, he shoved a bureau against the door. Then, with a sigh of despair, he threw himself down onto the gray and white ticking of a naked mattress. He lay there face-down for a moment, then rolled over and regarded the naked light bulb above him dangling from a cord.

It had all been a disaster, he thought. The entire afternoon had been one long catastrophe. Nothing had gone right. Just one long series of failures. He hadn't been able to locate his pusher, to begin with. Next, Sherm had refused to cooperate, and threatened him in the bargain. Then, one after another, his so-called friends had turned down his plea for a loan.

As he lay there, he could still almost hear their voices: "Sorry, Jimmy. I blew it all on presents . . ."

"Wish I could help you out, buddy, but I'm off to Boston tonight and I'll need every . . ."

"Not me, pal. Why I wouldn't lend a dime to my own mother. I'm just not the type. Why don't you try . . ."

"But you owe me twenty already, Jimmy . . ."

At the moment Jim felt no craving for a fix. But the very condition of possessing neither the makings nor the necessary money for one sent acids of anxiety through him.

He stirred about uneasily, trying and failing to find a more comfortable position on his bed.

What, he asked himself, could he do now? Where could he find enough money to fill his syringe — how many times? And once more he calculated the minimal requirements for the holidays. It wouldn't take a great deal of money, he assured himself. Fifty or sixty dollars ought to do it. Just enough to carry him through to the new year.

And after that?

The troublesome voice within that tossed out such questions had become all but silent these days. Still, when it did offer its unsolicited opinions, Jimmy was ready with the customary arguments and reassurances.

There was no sense in crossing that particular bridge until he came to it, he counseled that voice. He would worry about the new year when the time came. And, as a matter of fact, he already had a few resolutions in mind.

Resolutions?

Well, nothing specific as yet. But he had an idea or two.

Like?

Like quitting the drug routine. Like rejoining the straight world. Like settling down. Why, he might even go back to college! Or get a job! Yes, a real eight to five job. Of course it would have to be a job suitable to his talents. He wasn't interested in just *any* old job. Nothing common would do for the likes of Jim Mortimer. He needed something — well, something special. Something with class. Perhaps some sort of work connected with the stage. Something up on Broadway.

He conjured a vision. In his imagination he saw himself busily directing a play. A group of well-known actors and actresses were standing about in various postures of deference listening to what he had to say. He was clean and well-dressed now. The tracks along his inner arm had entirely disappeared. A penthouse apartment equipped with every imaginable luxury awaited him at home.

He pictured the situation with remarkable clarity. The

vision was so richly detailed, so palpable that he could almost reach out and touch it. What was more, it all seemed so easily attainable. All it required was a resolution or two — or so it seemed to Jimmy.

He did his best to elaborate the fantasy, to let it grow strong enough to provide him with a measure of escape from his present difficulties. But to no avail. The old dreams just didn't have the soothing power they once had. In recent months that golden future had become increasingly remote to Jimmy. He found that he was forced to take the measure of his life in daily increments now. His addiction prevented him from seeing much further than the limits of his financial or narcotic resources; and these, for the moment, were riveting his attention to this very day, this very Dec. 24. He needed drugs *now*, and drugs required money *now*, and fantasies about the future weren't of much help.

Jimmy abandoned the vision of himself as a successful Broadway director and refocused his mind on possible solutions to his current dilemma. As he considered the various possibilities remaining to him, he found himself returning again and again to one which had come to him with considerable regularity in recent days. Only this afternoon he had thought of it as he passed a gift shop near Washington Square. What it came to was the notion that a bit of discreet shoplifting might provide a temporary remedy to his financial problems.

Up until now Jimmy had never resorted to petty thievery to support his habit. He'd managed to get by so far on the basis of odd jobs, wheedled loans, and parental grants. He knew that shoplifting was a way of life with most addicts.

67

But hitherto he'd despised them for it and swore he'd never stoop to it himself.

And yet, on this Christmas Eve afternoon, the old resolves were becoming a bit fluid to Jimmy. As he lay there on his mattress, there occurred to him the thought that shoplifting might not be such a despicable enterprise after all. Indeed, viewed a certain way, shoplifting could almost be regarded as — well, as almost an *art*. What was *really* to be avoided, he noted to himself, was ordinary, grubby theft like raiding dime stores and supermarkets. Such activities were just plain stealing. But a deft bit of sleight-of-hand in a high-class store? That was something else again! Why, when one thought of the unconscionable profits made by these places, it was very nearly *commendable!*

The more Jimmy considered this particular answer to his problems, the more appealing it became.

And so, with such thoughts running through his mind, Jimmy set out.

By the time he reached Fifth Avenue, the stores were about to close. He walked past several, then settled for a department store in the vicinity of 51st Street.

It took Jimmy awhile to decide on something to be honored with his talents as a shoplifter. After rejecting a half dozen candidates, he chanced upon the very sort of thing he had been looking for. It was located among a display of several dozen cigarette lighters. The particular lighter which caught his eye was not the pocket variety, but a much more massive affair, designed to rest on a coffee table. The attached tag carried a price figure three times that of the others and, as if in explanation, had the word "sterling" lettered below.

The lighter was truly handsome. It presided over the

68

others like an aristocrat. Its rich, subdued metal luster was in itself a rebuke to the flashier, anodyzed inferiors all around it.

There were, however, other characteristics about the lighter which appealed to Jimmy. Although larger than most, the lighter was still small enough to be readily concealed. Furthermore, there would be no difficulty selling it. Its worth was self-evident.

Jimmy picked up the lighter and examined it. Later he would realize that this would have been the best time to make off with it. But for the moment something held him back. Pocketing it couldn't be *that* simple, he told himself. So he set the lighter back on the counter and began examining the others as though making comparisons.

No one seemed especially interested in what he was doing. He glanced several times in this direction and that. He noticed a saleslady down the way who was patiently engaged in demonstrating one cigarette lighter after another to a woman in a sheared lamb jacket. But beyond this there was no activity whatever in the near vicinity.

Jimmy went over his plan once more. He would pick up the lighter as if inspecting it. Then he would palm it. Next, concealed in his left hand, the lighter would be eased into his jacket pocket. At the same time he would be picking up another lighter with his right hand.

Easy enough, he told himself. Magician stuff. Attract attention with one hand. Let the other do what needed doing.

But still he hesitated. He found himself compelled to look around once more. For some reason his mouth had gotten terribly dry. Jimmy gulped several times. He licked his lips. He made a strenuous effort to appear nonchalant.

Then bad luck. A shopper moved into the area. This one

happened to be a man in a black topcoat who was carrying a briefcase in one hand and a peppermint-striped shopping bag in the other. He walked up beside Jimmy, looked over the same display of cigarette lighters, then turned his back and began to examine a collection of world globes on the counter across the aisle.

For Jimmy the time had come. Just one more quick survey of the area.

With a furtive look first one way and then the other, Jim reached for the lighter. He picked it up. He looked it over; then, with another quick survey of the area, enclosed it with his fingers. He felt the coldness of metal against the damp warmth of his palm. Now all he had to do was to pick up another lighter with his right hand and simultaneously slip the lighter into his left jacket pocket.

But before he could begin that part of it, he thought he heard the shopper behind him saying something.

Jimmy glanced around. As he did so, he moved the lighter closer to his waiting pocket.

It seemed rather odd to him, that voice. The man had obviously been talking aloud to the globes, for there was no one else around.

"Did you hear what I said?"

The voice was clearer now.

Jim paused. He turned yet further, and from the corners of his eyes carefully observed the shopper. All he could see was the man's back. It seemed so curious. The shopper seemed to be addressing him, and yet he was looking the other way. There was a riddle here, and no apparent answer.

Without letting go of the lighter, Jimmy inquired, "Who are you talking to? *Me?*"

"Yes, *you!*"

The words came out in two emphatic spurts. The man remained silent for a moment, then began again.

"I said, I'd hate to have to arrest anyone on Christmas Eve!"

Jimmy sagged.

"Huh?" he grunted.

As he did so, he suddenly caught sight of the man's face in the reflection of a tall glass case behind the counter. It all came clear. The man had been using the glass as a mirror. He'd been watching Jimmy all the time.

Jimmy pushed the sterling lighter back toward the others and let it go. Afterwards there was nothing to do but face the man.

He swung round. The man also was turning. The two closed on each other. The man's eyes searched out Jimmy's.

"But if I gotta arrest ya, I will," he said.

In his hand the man now held a wallet which he had flipped open, revealing a badge.

"What are you talking about, anyway?" Jimmy said, attempting bravado but making a bad show of it and realizing it.

"I'm talking about that seventy dollar lighter you were about to swipe."

"Swipe?"

"Yeah, swipe!"

"I wasn't trying to swipe any lighter!" Jimmy fumed.

"And just who are you tryin' to kid, anyway?" the man said. "I've been watchin' ya for the past five minutes. And there's something I gotta tell ya right away, and that is that you've got to be one of the dumbest shoplifters I ever seen. Anyone could tell a mile off what you've been up to."

"I wasn't shoplifting," Jimmy protested hotly. "I was just getting ready to buy one of these things, that's all."

"Buy one, eh? So what else have you *bought* today?" the man scoffed, nodding at Jimmy's jacket.

"I haven't bought *anything* else today! Nor stolen anything either, if that's what you mean. You can search me if you like," Jimmy said, and he began to turn his jacket pockets inside out.

The plainclothesman said nothing, but let him finish with all of his pockets. Except for one very dirty handkerchief and a few wads of paper, they were completely empty.

"So, if you were going to buy that lighter, what were you going to buy it *with,* buddy?"

"I . . . I . . . I . . ." Jimmy stuttered, embarrassed by the lack of any ready answer. "I wasn't going to buy it today anyway. After Christmas maybe, when it's on sale."

While he was struggling for an answer, the man took to examining Jimmy's face closely. When he found what he was searching for, the lines in his own face softened somewhat. Then he said quietly, "Why dontcha let that stuff alone, kid? I mean, what good is it? Where's it gonna getcha when you're old like me?"

By now the discussion had begun to gather a ring of shoppers. Their barely disguised curiosity embarrassed Jimmy. He felt loathsome and cheap.

"I don't know what the heck you're talking about," he spluttered. "Why are you picking on me, anyway? I don't

73

have anything! Can't you see that? Can't a person do any shopping around here without being set on by the house dicks?"

Mustering a look of indignation, Jimmy turned and stalked off.

The man let him go.

A counterful of men's wallets came up beside him. Jimmy stopped and examined a few as casually as he could. He noticed that the man had followed. He was making no secret of the fact that he was keeping Jimmy under observation.

Jimmy proceeded to costume jewelry. The man followed close behind.

Further along there appeared a row of glass exit doors. The brass casements of these doors were covered with a smudge composed of thousands of fingerprints. Jimmy broke toward them with a quick maneuver and added his own as he pushed out into the night.

His first few lungfuls of cold air left him with a giddy feeling. He'd escaped! He was free! Free at the very moment when he might have found himself being hurtled past the gaze of bystanders to some back office, there to be snared in a web of accusations from which there was no escape.

But it hadn't happened that way! He'd made it out of there! He'd beaten the rap! He'd fast-talked his way out of a bad situation! What luck! What utter, absolute, spectacular luck! Luck as pure as the flakes of Christmas snow which were beginning to fall now, and all because some slob of a store detective had made his move too soon, and followed that by either being too dumb or too lazy to carry out an arrest 10 minutes before quitting time.

Jimmy hadn't felt so good all day. The moments of fear had purged him. He felt clean now. He felt alive and unconquerable.

But, in this moment of elation, he felt something else too. Deep inside, Jimmy was beginning to sense the first stirrings of a devouring hunger. It touched his nerves like the pluck of a violin string. It sounded and was gone. But he knew it would return again with increasing insistence.

"What to do now?" Jimmy asked himself, walking faster than he needed to.

A bookstore materialized on his right. He entered and gradually made his way to the section on religion and philosophy. There was a book on Whitehead there. It reminded him that before dropping out of college he'd put up a brief struggle with Whitehead and lost.

After leaving the bookstore, he continued to make his way up Fifth Avenue. He stopped briefly by a window in which a dozen or so men's shoes were displayed against a background of green silk and dark walnut wainscoting. The shoes had such a bright gloss to them that Jimmy suspected they might have been sprayed with a transparent lacquer.

He turned and walked on. A little ways along he noticed that across the street a number of people seemed to be converging on a fixed point. From what he could see through the gauze of falling snow, it seemed to be a church.

Jimmy stepped over to the curb and stood there for a moment.

It was a church, all right. There beside it stood a glassed-in sign lighted with a fluorescent tube. The white plastic letters embedded in that sign informed passersby that Christmas Eve services were scheduled for 7:30 and 11 that evening. Below were the words of the sermon title.

THREE HEAVENLY GIFTS

Jimmy thought about churches for a moment.

Next his thoughts reverted to the subject of money.

Then he found himself thinking about these two together. Why? Because it suddenly occurred to him that there was rarely the one without the other. As one of his professors had told him, one was far more apt to find money in churches than religion. And it was true, come to think about it. There was always money in churches. Money in collection plates. Money in poor boxes. Money in purses. Money in wallets. Money under pew cushions. Money on tract tables. Money everywhere. Money just for the taking.

He crossed the street and entered the church. Inside he found a scattering of people. Jimmy scanned them for potential sources of revenue. In the process he happened to notice a smallish black boy sitting all by himself toward the rear of the church.

Jimmy briefly examined the boy's face as he made his way down the aisle. It was no more than a glance, a photograph of the mind. It took in the various components of vision — subject, space, dimension, texture, lightfall, perspective — and Jim snapped it and expected to forget it; or at most to file it along with countless other images of the mind stored deep within the memory like photos in an old and forgotten black-paged album, except that this particular snapshot would fall loose and confront him later on.

THE THIRD SHOP

Mrs. Lockroy's telephone call to the foremost jewelry establishment on Fifth Avenue was turned over to Emerson Gurney, the manager.

"Yes, madam," he said urbanely.

Mrs. Lockroy explained that she was calling to determine if the necklace advertised in such and so magazine had been sold as yet.

It is not surprising that Emerson Gurney immediately grew suspicious. Casual telephoned inquiries about major items of jewelry were not exactly the norm in his business, especially when they were made a few minutes before closing time on Christmas Eve. He found himself attacked by the vague feeling that either someone was playing a prank on him or he was about to be robbed.

"But we put out so *many* advertisements at this time of the year, madam," Mr. Gurney replied in a suave, noncommittal manner. "If you could be a bit more specific."

Mrs. Lockroy read the advertisement over the telephone.

"Oh, *that* necklace! Well, as a matter of fact, no. That particular necklace has not been sold as yet," Mr. Gurney told her. Nor, he added to himself, would it likely be sold in the foreseeable future at *that* price.

"Then would you be so good as to gift wrap it," Mrs. Lockroy promptly said. "I'll be right down to pick it up."

Mr. Gurney's left eye twitched slightly. But beyond

this no emotion showed in the distinguished lines of his face. He had trained himself to deal with every situation, however ordinary, however bizarre, with the same detached aplomb.

"Did I understand you to say that you would be right down?" Mr. Gurney asked.

"Yes. Just as soon as I can get downstairs and find a taxi."

"Get downstairs and find a taxi," echoed Mr. Gurney. "Yes . . . But madam, about the gift wrap . . ."

"It doesn't have to be anything special, you understand. I'm not fussy about that part of it. Anything will do. Whatever may be left there at the shop."

"Yes. I see. Whatever may be left here at the . . . *shop,* as you say. But before we discuss that part of it, madam, I wonder if you would mind telling me to whom I am speaking."

Mrs. Lockroy gave her name and address.

Mr. Gurney checked his memory.

"By any chance are you related to the Weatherstone Lockroys of Easthampton?" he asked.

Mrs. Lockroy allowed that she wasn't.

"That's too bad," said Emerson Gurney, a bit nonplussed and casting about for words. "But then again, perhaps it isn't. Depends on how one looks at these things, isn't that so? In any event, to get back to the — ah — gift wrapping, madam. Am I right when I assume that you are planning to give this necklace to someone as a Christmas gift?"

Mrs. Lockroy hesitated before answering.

"Well, yes. . . . In a sense," she said.

"A very choice gift, if I may say so, madam. You must have been considering it for a very long time."

"Well, no. The truth is that I just now thought of it."

"Just . . . *now?*"

"Well, five minutes ago."

"Five minutes ago," repeated Mr. Gurney, doubt flooding his mind. "How very interesting."

"Still I'm glad I thought of it before you closed," Mrs. Lockroy told him.

"A very happy thought, madam."

"It came to me all of a sudden. I remembered seeing the picture of it some time ago. And when I opened the magazine and looked again, I knew it was just the thing."

"Just the thing, yes," said Mr. Gurney, toying with the idea of replacing the receiver on its cradle and going about his business.

"You *will* have it ready for me, then?"

"About the gift wrapping . . ."

"I thought I already explained about that. It doesn't have to be anything fancy. Anything will do."

"It's not the *nature* of the wrapping that concerns me, madam. It's just — well, it's just that I wonder if you wouldn't prefer to *examine* the necklace before it's wrapped."

"Oh my no! That would take away the surprise!"

The tick in Mr. Gurney's left eye became reactivated.

"Did you say, 'Take away the surprise?' "

"Of course. People don't want to see their Christmas gifts before Christmas, do they?"

Mr. Gurney pondered the substance of her remarks for a few moments before speaking.

Then in measured tones he said, "I can see that as donor

you might want to share in such a splendid surprise as this, Mrs. Lockroy. But don't you think . . ."

"Gift wrapped," said Mrs. Lockroy firmly.

"Of course, if that's your preference. It's only that when one buys something in this price range sight unseen — well, what I mean to say is that it's practically unheard of."

"I can only assume that your firm is reliable," said Mrs. Lockroy a trifle stiffly.

"There has *never* been any question about *that,*" said Mr. Gurney with equal stiffness. "Since 1872 this firm has been the very *soul* of reliability. The point I am attempting to make, however, is that the style of the necklace might not be to your tastes, or the tastes of the recipient either. If you were only to *look* at it, you might be in a better position to judge."

"If it looks like the picture in the magazine," declared Mrs. Lockroy, "I shall be quite satisfied."

"I can assure you, madam, that it is exactly the same. The photo was in no way retouched."

"Then all you have to do is to wrap it as I suggested," said Mrs. Lockroy with an air of finality. "I'll be right down for it."

Emerson Gurney could not shake his confusion. For the most part he was inclined to believe that the person at the other end of the telephone line was playing a trick on him. And the truth of it is that Emerson Gurney was not in the mood for tricks. It had been a long, grueling Christmas season, and to cap it off by having this particular necklace removed from the safe and gift wrapped, only to lie unclaimed, would be humiliating in the extreme. Why, he told himself, the sales staff would snicker over that one for six months to come.

And yet there were certain aspects of this telephone call which caused him to wonder about the practical joke theory. Chief of them was the unbelievability of what he had heard. This Mrs. Lockroy, whoever she was, sounded too implausible to be untrue. And, if such were the case, Emerson Gurney did not want to risk losing what could very well be the sale of the season.

"Ah yes, madam. One other thing," said Emerson Gurney before Mrs. Lockroy had a chance to hang up.

"What now?"

"It's only that since it is so close to closing time, it would — ah — expedite matters here if you could tell me the — ah — manner in which you plan to pay for this necklace."

"Why, I'll charge it, I suppose," said Mrs. Lockroy, who up until this moment hadn't given this aspect of the matter much thought.

"Charge it, did you say?" Mr. Gurney said, leaning slightly further in the direction of the practical joke theory. "Am I to presume, then, that you have an account with us?" he asked, knowing full well that she did not.

"Oh dear! I don't think I do at that! I suppose I'll just have to make out a check."

"A check? A personal check?"

"Of course."

"Well, Mrs. Lockroy, I trust that you will not mistake my meaning. But I must tell you that it is a long-standing policy of our establishment, when personal checks involving sizable sums are involved, to consult with the bank involved. Unfortunately, in this instance, the banks are already closed."

82

"You aren't suggesting that I would write a bad check, are you?" said Mrs. Lockroy coldly.

"Oh no, madam! No, no, no, no, no. It's the very farthest thing from my mind. I'm just advising you of an ordinary business precaution we take with all our customers. It's a store policy, and not intended to reflect on the character of *anyone*. But let me say, madam, since we're on the subject of precautions, that there are other matters which require *your* attention as well. For example, there's the matter of insurance. I mean, after all, Mrs. Lockroy, we wouldn't want you walking out of here with an uninsured necklace of this excellence, would we?"

"Dear me! I suppose not," Mrs. Lockroy replied. "And the truth is I don't know a thing about insurance. My attorney sees to these matters."

Ah, said Mr. Gurney to himself, she has an attorney! *Now* we're getting somewhere!

"And what is his name, madam?"

"Whose name?"

"Your attorney's, madam."

"Why, Barnswallow."

"Y. *what*, madam?"

"Barnswallow."

"Swallow?"

"*Barn*swallow."

"Y. Barnswallow."

"No, not Y. Barnswallow. *John* Barnswallow."

"John Barnswallow, then. And with what firm might Mr. John Barnswallow be?"

"Grubbs Grubbs Walden and Barksdale, of course."

It was at the sound of these four names that Emerson

Gurney at least realized that he was dealing not with a prankster but a *bona fide* customer. And what was the reason for this? Simply that the legal firm of Grubbs Grubbs Walden and Barksdale, while not the most famous, was nevertheless the most select in all of Manhattan. Indeed, its preeminence had always been a well-kept secret, guarded most rigorously by the firm itself. It was a tradition of long standing in the firm of Grubbs Grubbs Walden and Barksdale that the legal affairs of its rich and well-born clientele be attended to with utmost discretion. Hence, the various partners of the firm functioned from within the cherry-paneled walls of their lower Broadway offices in an aura of virtual secrecy. Not five salesmen the length of Fifth Avenue knew the hidden prominence of Grubbs Grubbs Walden and Barksdale. But Emerson Gurney knew. And he acted accordingly. Within five minutes of concluding his chat with Mrs. Lockroy he had reached John Barnswallow at his New Canaan residence by telephone.

When this latter conversation had ended, Mr. Gurney strolled with customary dignity toward the rear of the main showroom. Here he encountered a metal lattice door which he unlocked and folded back accordion-fashion. On the other side was a flight of stairs which led down to the entrance of an enormous walk-in safe.

Mr. Gurney underwent a brief signing-in ceremony. Then he twisted a few dials, threw a switch, turned a great metal handle, and swung the great door open.

Inside, among the rows and rows of metal drawers, Mr. Gurney found the one he was looking for. He unlocked the metal flap which covered it, and from inside withdrew a long slender case.

A few moments later he had returned upstairs. He took the case to a counter where the most recent employee, a young man in his mid-20s, was standing. He opened the case under the young man's nose. He watched the widening eyes. He heard a sharp intake of breath.

Then Mr. Gurney snapped the case shut with a bang and threw it on the counter with as much disdain as he could muster.

"Here," he said to the young man. "Gift wrap it!"

"Gift wrap it, Mr. Gurney?"

"Gift wrap it," affirmed Mr. Gurney.

"But . . ." protested the young man feebly.

"Yes?" inquired Emerson Gurney coldly.

"But I'm not very good at gift wrapping yet, Mr. Gurney."

"It doesn't matter," Emerson Gurney replied as he began walking away. "Anything will do."

The store had closed and the sales staff were dismissed before Mrs. Lockroy arrived. Emerson Gurney, nevertheless, was on hand to admit her at the front door.

By this time Mrs. Lockroy had begun having second thoughts about the idea of giving herself a Christmas gift. What had seemed so very appropriate at the height of her anger now began to seem merely impulsive. She was especially bothered by the possibility of having to explain her actions. Because of this she had decided, on her way downtown, to keep her dealings with Mr. Gurney as businesslike as possible.

He stood at her side as she made out the check. He helped her get all the right numbers and words in the appropriate places. When she had finished, she waved the check around in the air so that the ink would dry. Emerson Gurney eyed the fluttering wisp of paper hungrily, but reached for it with due restraint when tendered.

He was still looking at the various inscriptions when it occurred to him that Mrs. Lockroy had already picked up the package, had murmured a holiday sentiment of some sort, and was already halfway to the door.

"Ah, Mrs. Lockroy," Mr. Gurney called out, waving a finger and hurrying after her.

She stopped and turned around.

"There's one thing I neglected to explain to you. What I mean is that we've arranged for a guard and limousine to see you home," he said.

"Did you say a limousine?" asked Mrs. Lockroy.

Emerson Gurney nodded.

"And a guard?"

He nodded again.

"With a uniform and a gun and that sort of thing?"

"Naturally, madam. When we *say* a guard, we *mean* a guard!"

"Whatever would I want with all that, when a taxi would do just as well?" protested Helen Lockroy.

"But Mrs. Lockroy, I insist!" said Mr. Gurney soothingly. "Really, Mrs. Lockroy. This is a customary procedure when people take from the store items of this — ah — magnitude."

Helen Lockroy returned a dubious look.

"There's no charge," he assured her, lest she happened to be one of those rich eccentrics who was extravagant in some ways and penurious in others.

"Thank you, but don't trouble yourself," said Mrs. Lockroy, and once more she headed for the door.

"But . . . but Mrs. Lockroy!" exclaimed Mr. Gurney.

"There are *people* out there!"

"People?" said Mrs. Lockroy looking puzzled. "Of course there are people."

"I mean purse-snatchers! Muggers! Pickpockets! Thugs! You're not safe out there! That necklace is apt to be stolen. Someone might just — well, just *snitch* it right out of your hands! So, for your own good, you must, you simply *must* let us see that you are taken home properly!"

Mrs. Lockroy looked through the store window at the people walking by. Her eyes next rose to a clock on the wall overhead. It was, she realized, getting quite late.

With the accumulation of wealth, there had come to Mrs. Lockroy the ability to speak quite positively when the need arose. Such a time, to her way of thinking, had now come. She set her chin. She narrowed her eyes. She tapped the floor with one foot. Then, in a few extremely positive phrases, she informed Emerson Gurney that he no doubt wished to get right home to be with his family on this Christmas Eve. Because of this, she had no intention whatever of detaining him — or anyone else, for that matter. It would be no problem for her, she told him, to walk outside and hail a taxi. As for the danger of the necklace being stolen, it was not, after all, as though she were wearing it outside her fur coat. The necklace, she felt, was quite secure in its wrapping. After all, didn't the package look like nearly every other package being carried about on this Christmas Eve? Surely it was as safe in her hands on this night as if being borne about in the presence of armed men. She concluded by suggesting that Mr. Gurney think no more on the subject, bade him a Merry Christmas, and walked briskly out of the store.

Once out on the street, Mrs. Lockroy had some difficulty

in attracting the attention of a cab driver. She raised her arm in appropriate New York fashion, forefinger extended, but nothing came of it. The taxis hurried by, signal lights out or off-duty signs displayed on the windshield.

All this time people were brushing by her as they hurried to be here or there.

As she waited, it amused her to think that none of these people realized that the small package which she held so casually in her hand contained a string of such valuable gems. So far as the passersby were concerned, the package could just as well contain slippers or chocolates.

While standing by the curb, something in one of the show windows across the street attracted Mrs. Lockroy's attention. She walked to the intersection, crossed over and then began walking down Fifth Avenue against the general flow of pedestrian traffic.

No sooner had she reached the other side, however, than she realized that she had quite forgotten what it was she had come over to see. She made a halfhearted attempt at remembering, but couldn't, so gave up the effort.

She was walking rather aimlessly now. As she moved through the crowds, her thoughts reverted once more to the package she held in her hand. The wrapping was, she noted once more, so very ordinary. The contents, by contrast, were so extraordinary! How very droll, she told herself, to be misleading all these people around her! And how very exciting! It was rather like a game!

Mrs. Lockroy now began dangling the package by its ribbon as though daring those who passed by to jostle it from her hand and send it crashing to the street. It was positively reckless! She had never been so daring before!

She felt exhilarated by her actions and could not help noticing that all of her feelings of bitterness and loneliness were quite gone now. She knew that she was acting like an unloved child flaunting an expensive toy, but she didn't care.

Unfortunately for Mrs. Lockroy, she had not reckoned with her deepest emotions. One does not live a life of caution and abruptly give oneself over to abandon without tripping the various alarms of the mind.

And so it was that Helen Lockroy became the victim of a severe attack of anxiety. As she walked along, she began to notice that her feelings of exhilaration were gradually changing into a curious giddiness. She wasn't sure she liked this particular sensation, but hardly had time to evaluate the matter when the giddiness evolved into a decided light-headedness.

Then, with horrifying suddenness, there came to her the conviction that she was about to faint. She felt the blood drain from her face. She heard the characteristic buzz in the ears. She experienced a watery sensation in her knees.

Mrs. Lockroy stopped and leaned against a sheet of cold plate glass. She saw her distress mirrored in the face of a man who turned to look at her before hurrying on.

She wasn't quite sure what to do next.

After a moment or two she tried a few unsteady steps. Then she felt obliged to stand still once more. The prospect of collapsing on the streets of Manhattan — the embarrassment of it more than anything else — was what seemed to bother her the most. But then, could she avoid it? Already she felt as though she were in the process of suffocating. At the moment she was gasping for air. Her heart had quickened to the crisis and was thudding away inside her like a kettle-drum.

Even more ominous was the manner in which the noises of the street had begun to grow indistinct. Slowly they were turning into a terrible, undifferentiated roar. She tried to sort them out in her mind — the traffic, the voices, the ampli-fied music — but it was no good. They were too intermingled, too confused, too overwhelming.

But then, just as she was beginning to wonder how much more of this chaotic noise she could take, there came to her, in gentle counterpoint, the sound of an organ.

She looked up. She strained for its source and feared she might not find it, when perchance she caught sight of the door of a nearby church gliding shut. As the door closed, the rich organ sounds faded and ceased.

Her heart was beating faster now. A wash of cold per-spiration lay against her forehead. There had come upon her a desperate longing for refuge. In her condition she wanted to hide herself. And that church, she now realized, was where this ought to happen.

But first there remained the problem of getting there.

She looked at the granite steps which led to the church doors and calculated the distance. Not 200 feet, she estimated.

"You can get that far," she murmured to herself.

She began shuffling forward, balancing herself against the glass of a shop window.

The mannequins within seemed to respond with gestures of alarm. Their outstretched arms, their palms turned grace-fully upwards, their thin beckoning fingers as much as said, "Behold this person struggling for a place to rest!"

By the time Mrs. Lockroy had reached the steps leading to

the church, her faintness had become complicated by a feeling of nausea. She raised a foot to the first step and pulled the other beside it. As she did so, she began talking to herself.

"Come on, Helen! Up the steps now! Don't be in a hurry, though! Just take them one at a time!"

At first the ascent seemed impossibly high. But she countered her despair by reminding herself of all the things she'd ever been told about will power and, before she'd gotten halfway through, found herself two thirds of the way up the stairs.

"All right, Helen! Just a few more to go!" she advised herself.

She stopped a few moments to clear her head, then struggled on.

"Now, then, through the door and . . . oh dear! Another door! But you're almost there, so don't fret. Just pull the handle! That's it! But you must hurry now, dear! That usher is coming toward you. He'll make a scene if he sees how bad off you are! Here in the back is good enough! Just slide along the pew and . . ."

And with these last few words of encouragement Helen Lockroy sat down and leaned far forward as though in an attitude of prayer.

Gradually the sensations of the world returned to her — the varnished oak against which her forehead rested, the velvet pew cushions with their taut round buttons sunk into the fabric, the slats of the hymnal rack, the rustle of worshipers' clothing, the fluted softness of that very organ on which she had homed, the suede texture of the leather of her purse, the stiff sharp edges of the ribbon which bound her very own Christmas gift.

She began to assess her condition. What, she wondered, had happened to her out there? Had she suffered a seizure of some kind? a stroke? a heart attack?

Well, she counseled herself, there was no telling. All that mattered at the moment was that she get a little rest. All she needed now was to get hold of herself so that she could get home and call the doctor.

She took a measure of comfort from the fact that she hadn't collapsed on the street. She pictured herself lying outside with a circle of curious onlookers around her. She could almost hear their murmurs, almost imagine one of those terrible Knickerbocker ambulances, which must surely shake the life out of anyone who managed to survive an accident, coming to collect her.

When a few minutes had gone by without any further complications, she tried moving a hand. That seemed to work all right, so she tried the other. Her legs too, when she moved them, seemed in working order once more.

It was all very encouraging. She seemed on the mend now.

Looking to one side, she saw that if she were to move further to her left she would become somewhat concealed in the shadow of a pillar.

This possibility seemed fine to her. She told herself that if her time to die had come, it would be ever so much better to die in some unnoticed and darkened place, die discreetly and be discovered by the sexton at closing time, than making a spectacle of herself out in the open.

Ever so gently she maneuvered herself along the pew

toward this place of concealment. Once in its shadows, she began to feel better still.

After awhile she turned sideways and began watching the worshipers as they came in. She noticed how they tiptoed with furtive, guilty glances in the direction of the altar, how abject they seemed and afraid.

In the process, she also happened to observe, among all of these immaculately clad sinners, a small black boy who had seated himself in the same row as herself, though nearer the center aisle.

As Mrs. Lockroy examined the lad, she noted, somewhat idly, that he was carrying a package which seemed to be about the same size as hers. And not that only, it also appeared to be wrapped in very much the same way — gold paper tied with a gold ribbon.

WHAT THE PREACHER SAID

A procession signaled the beginning of it all. It appeared from some mysterious recess of the church, led by a silver processional cross and two flickering tapers held aloft. There followed a double column of acolytes and choristers and clergy swaying to some unheard music — or, at least, certainly not that of the organ.

On and on they came until they reached that central part of the church known as the crossing. There they turned in the direction of the altar, rose up the chancel steps like a stream of ghosts, then began to dissipate to their various appointed places.

The sermon came rather near the beginning of the Christmas liturgy. The preacher, when he came forward, seemed a rather timid chap. He limped along with an apologetic slope to his shoulders and, when he came to stand in the pulpit, one could hardly say that he filled it. To make matters worse, his sermon was delayed for no inconsiderable time while the choir was completing the various and sundry "amens" of an anthem. The result was that there was nothing for the poor man to do but stand there awkwardly, fingers working nervously at his manuscript, pince-nez twinkling and trembling on the brink of his nose, surplice gushing from his shoulders like a fountain of milk.

"A-a-a-a-amen-n-n," bawled the choir. "Amen, amen, amen. *Amen!* A-a-a-a-amen-n-n. AMEN! AMEN!! AMEN!!!

Amen. Amen. Amen. amen. amen. amen. A-a-a-a-a-a-A-A-A-A-a-a-a-a-men-n-n-n-N-N-N-N-n-n-n-n."

When at last the music died away, the clergyman cleared his throat and announced that the title of his sermon was "Three Heavenly Gifts," the which, it will be recalled, tallied with the information on the announcement board outside. His text, he informed the congregation, was taken from the famous 13th chapter of First Corinthians: "And now abideth faith, hope, charity, these three; but the greatest of these is charity."

In certain respects the sermon proved to be a model of homiletic structure. For example, there was a relentless threeness to it — three points, three subpoints, three motifs, three symbols thrice. Indeed, the trinitarian character of all that was said should have satisfied, if no one else, the granite hearts of those various ancient masters of preaching who had been carved into the walls of the pulpit — Justin and Clement, Irenaeus and Basil, Chrysostom and Augustine.

The preacher began by reminding the congregation of the return of that season when minds became preoccupied with the giving of gifts. Such an activity, he noted, seemed a trait peculiar to human beings. He observed that humanity's lesser relations in the animal world seemed bent on *taking* things from one another — sometimes by deception, sometimes by stealth, sometimes by force. The preacher admitted that humans also shared in this unhappy tendency. But that was not the sum of it, for humans also possessed this odd penchant for giving things, and often gave in the most outrageous and unexpected ways.

How did one explain such an unusual phenomenon?

The preacher answered his own question by suggesting

that the giving of gifts in some measure reflected man's divine origins. For God too gave gifts, gave them in abundance and variety. All sorts of gifts were constantly being showered upon mankind from above, gifts both great and small, measurable and immeasurable, material and spiritual.

As an instance of the latter, the preacher averted to St. Paul's catalog of heavenly gifts: faith, hope, and charity. Here were gifts, the preacher claimed, which were quite priceless.

The clergyman nevertheless supposed that, on the whole, people would prefer the gifts of men rather than those of God. One was apt to be far more intrigued with the gold, frankincense, and myrrh given by the Wise Men than the faith, hope, and charity given by the wise God. This was apparently so not only because human beings tended to have a penchant for material things, but also because they were not entirely convinced about the true worth of the spiritual gifts available to them.

The gift of faith, for example, was frequently regarded as being little more than outright credulity. Here the clergyman quoted Samuel Butler's definition of faith as the believing of things which people knew to be untrue.

And yet, the preacher claimed, faith properly understood could hardly be regarded as self-delusion. Rather, the heavenly gift of faith was nothing less than the confidence that the universe was in good hands (which at once ruled out the possibility that it might be in bad hands or no hands at all). Faith was the belief that all creation was suffused with meaning. Faith was the conviction that the world had been intended for some great and good purpose. Faith was the assurance that all persons, however pleasurable or painful their lot, however noble or depraved their actions, however abundant or meager their means, could always lay claim to some small share in that purpose if they so desired.

The preacher said that if faith were understood this way, men and women might realize that the alternative to faith was not so much doubt as a sense of emptiness and despair. Without confidence in a good and loving God, one was left with nothing to believe in but oneself — the which, in the preacher's opinion, was a rather pathetic substitute. He then went on to explain that the act of exchanging faith in oneself for faith in God had traditionally been called repentance. For this reason the gift of faith often came only after one was forced to take a long and painful look at oneself.

A second heavenly gift, the preacher went on, was hope. Men, unfortunately, could never seem to get this gift straight either, for most tended to suppose that hope amounted to little more than wishful thinking. The clergyman admitted that there might be a measure of truth here, and quoted Unamuno's remark about the first element of religion being the devout wish that there *was* a God. Hope, nevertheless, could always be distinguished from wishful thinking in that the latter merely floated. Wishful thinking was never attached to its object by anything real. Hope, by contrast, was always bound in some material way to that which was hoped for.

Lastly the preacher expounded on the gift of charity. Humans, he said, misunderstood this gift as much as the others, for they imagined charity to be the occasional practice of philanthropy. The preacher demurred. The charity which was the third of the heavenly gifts alluded to by the apostle was, he claimed, far more than casual benevolence. Indeed,

97

the charity which God presented to the willing heart was nothing less than a constant, unflagging compassion for others. Among other ways, charity sometimes manifested itself as an impulsive generosity which enabled a person not to hesitate throwing his most valued possession into the midst of human need, much as God once cast His Son into the world with such reckless abandon.

All in all, it was not a bad sermon. Even though the preacher broke every rule of elocution, even though he spoke barely above a whisper and hardly ever raised his eyes from the manuscript, one could detect in his utterances certain fruits of labor and of prayer.

The only trouble was that so few seemed to listen. Hardly had the preacher announced the text than eyes (and minds, presumably) began to wander. Indeed, it would be no exaggeration to suggest that only the All-Hearing One Himself listened to that sermon in its entirety. Certainly Mrs. Lockroy didn't, for she was much too concerned with the state of her health. Neither did young Jim Mortimer, whose drug-starved mind was preoccupied with the plotting of a theft. Nor yet did Rosie, who, as previously noted, had fallen asleep long before the sermon ever began.

A BIT OF
CHRISTMAS WHIMSY

For Rosie it began with the sensation that he was about to topple forward off the pew. He caught himself, jerked upright, and looked around. For a moment or two he wondered where he might be. Then the sound of the organ reminded him.

He noticed that the worshipers in his immediate vicinity seemed to be getting up from their places and moving forward. Without thinking much about it, Rosie concluded that he ought not to be a conspicuous exception to this procedure, whatever it might be. So he stood up, edged himself to the aisle, and joined the procession.

The aisle ended in an abbreviated flight of steps. Beyond lay an expanse of polished stone at the far end of which people were kneeling down.

Rosie stopped. He was still a bit dazed by his sleep and its abrupt termination. Yet he was sufficiently awake to realize that there were no children among the various kneelers, and he concluded that the activity being engaged in — and he had no inkling of what it might be — was probably not for him. Rosie then turned aside and made his way toward one of the side aisles.

He intended to double back toward his place at the rear of the church, and was about to do so when his attention became drawn to a Nativity display which had been set up near one of the side altars.

The manger scene had been artfully constructed. It rested on a raised platform covered by a green undulating fabric which suggested the hills of Judea. The three-sided shed at its center lacked siding, so that one could conveniently peer in at the creche and its wondrous occupant from any angle. All around were the other well-known figures of that story, all glazed and fired into positions of adoration — shepherds and angels, sheep and donkeys and cows, Mary and Joseph.

Rosie was utterly enchanted by the sight of it. With all children he shared a fascination for miniature replicas of human beings. They provided for him a scale of life over which he felt some measure of control. Thus there came over him an irresistible urge to rearrange the figures, to place them in positions more congenial to his remembrance of the Christmas story. Ever so slowly a finger stole out and touched a shepherd. The shepherd responded by teetering back and forth and threatening to fall down. Rosie immediately decided that there was a do-not-touch air about the display which had better be heeded.

All this while Jim Mortimer had been busily attempting to get his hands on some money. One opportunity had arisen earlier in the service. This was when the collection plates had been passed. Nothing, however, had come of it. The truth was, there hadn't been sufficient time. All he had been able to do was glance into the plate and helplessly observe the fact that there were a few folded bills within an inch or two of his fingertips. The problem had been the gimlet eyes of the usher, which had focused upon Jimmy's hand as though intent on measuring the accumulation of dirt under the fingernails. Under the circumstances all Jimmy had been able to do was feign the dropping of a coin onto that little heap of money and reluctantly pass the plate along into the importunate, reaching hands of the person sitting next to him.

Nothing, then, had come of that first opportunity. But another was soon to come. Having been raised in such a church as this, Jim realized that toward the end of the service, people would be going forward to receive Communion. His remaining hope came to center on the possibility that out of all those communicants, one would likely walk up to the altar without remembering to take her purse, or leave his wallet tumbled out onto the pew cushion. If such were to happen, it would be a simple matter of appropriation, of finders keepers, losers weepers. All that was needed to pick up some money in this manner was some way of inspecting the vacated pews without seeming too obvious about it.

Jimmy pondered this matter during the long prayers which preceded the Communion. Before they ended, he had come up with what seemed to him a most satisfactory solution. What he would do was assume the role of the uncertain communicant. This meant that Jimmy would pretend that he was a person who could not make up his mind about receiving the Sacrament. He would start out confidently with each group of communicants as they made their way to the altar. But before ascending the chancel steps, he would stop. Then, as though uncertain of the state of his soul, he would turn back. By this method he would be able to keep walking up and down the main aisle, inspecting the just-vacated pews for any possessions which might be left behind.

And so he did. He began mingling with the worshipers

101

as they emptied the rows of pews by twos and threes and went forward. But each time, before reaching the Communion rail, he drifted to a halt. Then, feigning deep inner struggle, he stood there a moment. Finally, with many genuflections and signs of the cross, he turned about and made his way toward the rear of the church. As he walked back, he glanced down this row and that looking for purses or billfolds left behind.

Once more, however, Jimmy's expectations went unfulfilled. The worshipers in this church were as prudent as they were pious, leaving nothing behind them which was apt to be stolen. True, from time to time Jimmy *did* notice something out of the ordinary lying on a pew cushion. This would send him sidling toward it for a closer examination. But each time he found nothing more promising than ladies' handkerchiefs or personal prayer books bound in leather. And since these, he knew, were utterly worthless, he left them where he found them.

In his frustration Jimmy found himself growing strangely irritated by the worshipers there in that church. He resented their affluence, their religiosity, their failure to meet his expectations. These church people, he told himself, were supposed to love and trust everybody. But look how they clutched their possessions when they went forward to partake of the bread of charity! And with such thoughts as these he once more dismissed the entire religious enterprise as one vast sham.

For the fifth time, then, he was walking down the aisle in the company of all these hypocrites. For the fifth time he stopped before the altar as though uncertain of his worthiness. For the fifth time he wheeled round and mingled with those in the process of returning from the altar rail. For the fifth time he drew abreast of the emptied pews and began inspecting them for something of value left behind. For the fifth time nothing. Nothing, nothing, nothing. Just an expanse of comfortable pews!

The sight of them was beginning to disgust him. He felt despair in the pit of his stomach. His only comfort derived from his assumption that he was, after all, doing rather well as an actor. No one, he believed, had the least idea of what he was doing there. He looked round and assessed the situation once more. He estimated that there would be at least three more migrations of worshipers to the altar. There was, he encouraged himself, still hope. Not much, admittedly. But enough to keep up the act!

Jimmy, however, was not entirely correct in his supposition that no one in the church had perceived his intent. His act hadn't fooled everyone. To be sure, most of the people there were much too preoccupied with their own thoughts to pay any attention to him. Nor were they to be blamed for that. His only need, from a casual inspection, seemed to be a haircut. And yet, despite this general disregard, there did happen to be *one* person in that congregation who knew what Jimmy was up to, one who, among all the others, had come to discern Jimmy's true intentions. That person was Helen Lockroy.

By now she had quite recovered from her mysterious malady. She had even begun to take an interest in the doings forward. Not familiar with these particular rites, she had taken to watching both officiants and worshipers with the detached eye of an onlooker. In the course of this, she had come to notice that a certain young man seemed to be nearly everywhere at once — now at the chancel steps, now roaming the aisles, now side-slipping down a row of pews.

Her curiosity aroused, she began giving this young man her undivided attention. Almost at once, she discerned the truth of it. The young man, she realized, was a thief who was in the process of looking for purses left behind.

Mrs. Lockroy had never seen a thief at work before. She knew that there were thousands of them in the city. Thievery was a constant source of discussion among her friends. Nearly all of them seemed to be having their purses snatched or their apartments rifled these days. In fact, it wasn't so long ago that someone had attempted to force her own apartment door and, while failing in the attempt, had left great gouge marks along the jamb. Still, Helen Lockroy had never actually seen a thief going about his trade, and the result was that she found herself quite fascinated by it all.

To her surprise, she did not feel particularly outraged by the young man's actions. Her attitude was more one of curiosity than anything else. She found herself wondering if he would be able to succeed in his efforts, and it was this that kept her from alerting one of the ushers. She felt confident that if the young man *did* pick up something, it would not be at all difficult to signal someone.

Most important of all, she found herself being provided with a wealth of conversational material. Why, there was enough here to hold up her end of the chatter for years to come. Phrases were already forming in her mind.

"Right there in church, I tell you . . . Just as cool as you please . . . Absolutely brazen about it . . . Just walking up and down the aisle looking for something to steal . . ."

It was, as already noted, the last rows of communicants which drew Rosie in their wake.

Jimmy watched them go. He realized now that it would be useless to go through the charade yet another time. He was sick of it, anyway. Sick of acting and despairing of any success. Not 15 minutes ago the idea had seemed so promising. But now it was seen to be in the pattern of everything else he had tried that day — illusory and empty. The time had come, he felt, to leave this place. There was nothing here for him. All he could do at this point was to take a few last looks, then walk out into a darkness which contained the wards of Bellevue and the agonies of withdrawal.

He glanced down the length of one pew, then another. By this time he had reached the rearmost portion of the nave. Only two or three rows to go.

Another look. Nothing. He swiveled his head. Still nothing.

A few steps now and he would be at the door leading to the vestibule. He admitted defeat with a shrug of the shoulders, and had already started for the door when there came into the edges of his vision the glint of gold. Jimmy stopped. He backed up a few steps. He craned his neck.

Sure enough! Something with a decidedly golden cast to it lay on a pew not far away. From where he was standing, it appeared to Jimmy to be a package of some sort.

Jimmy edged closer. He could see now that his surmise had been correct. A package in Christmas wrapping lay on a pew cushion, and an expensive-looking package at that! Better yet, there was no one around.

Jimmy's heart soared. All that waiting! All those expectations! All that acting! They had, at last, come to something!

What luck! he exclaimed to himself. What boundless luck! He had all but given up, and then at the last moment his hunch had paid off. Twice lucky tonight! First in escaping from that stupid store detective. Now in finding in one of the last pews of a church an elegant package just aching to be picked up!

Quickly Jimmy sidestepped toward the package. As he closed on it, he became aware of some movement nearby. Looking up, he saw a woman seated a few yards beyond. She was motioning at him. They were feeble, warding-off motions. But by now he was past caring. He swept the package off the cushion, thrust it under his jacket and, without so much as a backward look, turned and sped from the church.

Helen Lockroy remained behind quite benumbed by this turn of events. The quickness and determination of the thief had very nearly paralyzed her. All her resolves, all her brave intentions to signal the ushers in the event the young man found something to steal — all of these had come to nothing. To be sure, she hadn't been prepared for the manner in which the thief literally pounced on that package — or so she attempted to reassure herself. And he had seemed so desperate about it! The eyes! It had been frightening to look into eyes like that! Why, they were the eyes of a trapped animal! No wonder he hadn't paid the least attention to her when she had waved her hand at him and tried (and failed) to cry, "Stop!"

"Oh dear," she at last murmured aloud. "Now he's gone and taken that little boy's package!"

She could not avoid the sense of her own responsibility for what had just happened; and this, in turn, made her quite angry with herself. Why, she demanded to know, hadn't she alerted the ushers the moment she realized what the young man was doing there in church? The thought occurred to her that there might still be time for one of them to collar the thief outside, but she had no trouble dismissing it. There was, she knew quite well, no possibility of that at all. The thief was doubtless blocks away by now. And all that could be expected from any explanation to the ushers was the possibility of some rather embarrassing questions. So she forsook this avenue of consideration for the more immediate problem of how to deal with the boy when he returned.

At that very moment Rosie was concluding his examination of the creche. He found himself somewhat puzzled at the rendering of the child in the manger. The *whiteness* of the child! The stark, porcelain whiteness! A whiteness reinforced by a crown of golden curls! He couldn't understand it. He recalled that his mother had once told him that Jesus was born in Africa. Or, if not in Africa, at least very near it, and somehow that fact did not square with the infant's fairness.

He found himself wishing, he didn't know why, that the child might look a little more like one of his younger sisters when she was a baby. And suddenly it was almost as if that wish were granted, for there seemed to come to him the sound of faint chimes, and the baby darkened somewhat and shone most lustrously and almost quivered with life. Rosie blinked in amazement and rubbed his eyes. But when he looked again, lo, it was the same bone-white child.

Heaving a great sigh, Rosie turned and started back to his place. He walked down the side aisle thumping his hand along the ends of the pews and, when he came abreast of his own, found himself obliged to squeeze past a woman who was sitting in the shadow of a pillar. He didn't bother to excuse himself, since she seemed to be in the process of sitting down anyway. He continued on toward his place, a place which he had no difficulty identifying, for his mother's package lay there on the cushion precisely where he had left it.

Rosie picked up the package and laid it on his lap. He may have wondered, briefly, if it did not seem a little heavier than before, but there was no more to it than that.

Mrs. Lockroy, in the meantime, was in the process of questioning her sanity.

"What in the world have you done, Helen Lockroy?" she asked herself severely. "What's come over you anyway, putting your package over there like that? You've taken leave of your senses, that's what! You've simply taken to acting like a crazy woman! All the fault of that business in the street, no doubt! You've let it get the better of you! And *now* look at the predicament you've made for yourself!"

Several minutes of this did not prove markedly helpful, so she tried another tack. She declared to herself that the only reasonable course of action now was to recapture her impulse. And that, she assured herself, would not be at all difficult. All it would take was a bit of explanation. Surely the boy was old enough to understand a simple explanation! Especially if it were reinforced by a few coins. Or even a dollar bill! That would be more than enough to salve the child's feelings and pay for whatever happened to be in that other package besides.

This matter settled, she returned to the bewilderment she felt at the rashness of her actions.

"Think of it!" she told herself. "Just rushing over there

like a madwoman and putting my own package where the other one had been!"

She wondered what Elwood would think of it all, and solemnly resolved to discuss the matter with him at the first opportunity. He would laugh, she knew. He would laugh and say that she'd never done anything like it in her life before, which was absolutely true.

Her reply would be that the giddiness had caused it. That would be reason, and reason enough. And if he pressed her, why she might even say something about her suspicion that the package had been the little boy's Christmas present to his mother.

How she had fastened onto this possibility she could not say. It had simply touched her like a flake of snow on the cheek, and then promptly turned into an iron conviction. She became *certain* that such was the case. This poor child, she informed herself without leaving any tolerance for doubt whatever, had come downtown to buy something for the dearest person in his life. And that person could be none other than his mother. Nor could Helen Lockroy keep from remembering, at this point, that she too was a mother, only in her case she'd been forgotten this Christmas Eve. And so she could explain to Elwood that, besides the faintness, certain maternal feelings had gone into all this foolishness, and he certainly wouldn't blame her for *that*!

Ah well, she thought, however she would handle Elwood, the time had come to retrieve the package. Quite likely, she told herself with a sidelong glance, the boy would show some reluctance at being asked to give up the package. Already he had fully assumed that it was his own. Why, at this very moment he was curling the ribbon round his fingers!

"All right, Helen," she advised herself, "delay can only make things worse. Move over now and explain what happened. Just tell the truth of it as simply as you can. Open your purse while you're doing it. Take out a dollar bill and hold it where he can see it. Or even two, if that's what it takes. But, at the same time, be firm with the lad. Don't take no for an answer. Make him understand what it is you're trying to say. Above all, don't get rattled and take to grabbing, or you'll have a scene on your hands. Just explain. Explain, explain, explain. And if he balks, tell him to open the package and see for himself. But hurry now! You've wasted too much time already . . . . *Look!* He's getting up to go! *He's on his way out!* "

And indeed he was. Rosie had reached the center aisle and was already making for the doors.

Mrs. Lockroy arose and hurried through the side vestibule door. She headed the boy off before he reached the outside doors.

"Little boy! Little boy!" she called.

Rosie stopped as though pierced by a dart which had been dipped in all the venoms of guilt. His various misdeeds rose up before him. He had touched the shepherd, remember? And he had been sleeping in church! And he had neglected to take off his cap until someone had motioned to him about it. And he was late getting started for home. Very late! And besides all this, he was out of place here. This was a place for grown-ups, and white grown-ups at that! And because of this, and ever so much more, accusations were apt to come from almost anywhere!

"The package," the woman was saying. She towered above him and seemed to be reaching for it.

Rosie pulled the package to his breast and attempted to conceal it with the cloth of his sleeve.

"It's mine," he said.

"Did someone *give* it to you?" Mrs. Lockroy asked. She bent down so that she could see his face beneath the bill of his cap.

"Bought it," said Rosie stubbornly.

"*Bought* it?" said the woman in what sounded to Rosie like a most skeptical voice. "With your own money?"

Rosie did not like the drift of the questions. There was something ominous about them. There was a threat to his mother's gift somewhere in them. They seemed to question his proprietorship, his right to own the package which he held so tightly, and with it there came the additional fear that any protestations to the contrary would somehow prove too feeble. He nevertheless nodded an affirmation. He *had* bought it with his own money, no matter what anyone said.

"What's your name, little boy?"

It was getting worse. It always meant real trouble when anyone asked his name. He pronounced it rapidly in an undertone.

"What did you say?" the woman said, her warm minted breath rushing past his face.

"Roosevelt," he said faintly.

"Roosevelt? Roosevelt *what* ?" she asked in what sounded to him like the epitome of doubt.

"Sims."

"Roosevelt Sims?"

Rosie nodded.

"And that package . . .?"

"It's for my mom," said Rosie, sounding both fearful

111

and defensive at the same time. "Bought it with my own money. Didn't steal it any."

The woman didn't answer right away. She was looking at a pair of sleeves which were much too short for a boy's arms.

Rosie mustered enough courage to inspect the expression on Mrs. Lockroy's face. To him the face had the unpleasant angularity of most white faces — all pinched and wrinkled and pointed, with scarlet spots and sharp edges and abrupt turns.

"Of course you didn't steal it," said Mrs. Lockroy at last. She looked thoughtful. "But listen to me, Roosevelt . . . . *Roosevelt!* Are you listening?"

"Yeah," said Rosie faintly toward the bottom edge of the fur.

"Someone almost *did* steal that package! Are you listening to me?"

Rosie nodded.

"You shouldn't just leave packages sitting around. There are bad people here in the city. People who steal things. You know that, don't you?"

"Yeah," said Rosie, hoping that she didn't think that he was one of them.

"Where do you live, Roosevelt?"

"A hundred seventeenth," said Rosie, looking down at her fur-lined rubber boots.

"Is that where you're going?"

"Yeah."

"That's a long ways off. Do you know the way?"

Rosie nodded.

"And do you have bus fare?"

Rosie nodded.

And will you promise me that you won't let go of that package until you put it into your mother's hands?"

Rosie nodded.

"Say, 'I promise!' "

"Promise."

"Well, then," said Mrs. Lockroy, and she paused a moment and listened to the sounds of the organ which had begun to beat against the doors of the church in a frantic effort to be free, "Well, then," she said once more, "I guess there's nothing more to say but . . . good-bye, Roosevelt. . . . Good-bye. And merry Christmas!"

And without so much as the beginning of a reply, Rosie pushed through the oaken door as though it were made of a sheet of cardboard, descended the steps two at a time and ran for the bus stop on the other side of the avenue.

And although he didn't know it, he was shadowed all the way to the bus stop by an aged lady with blue hair, two dabs of rouge on her cheeks, and the fur of mink about her shoulders. And she stood guard over him in a downdraft of the astonishing snowflakes of a Christmas Eve until she saw him step into a bus and pass from sight in a pattern of lighted bus windows which flickered by her like the frames of an old movie in the direction of uptown.

THE FIRST GIFT

Jim Mortimer was the first of the three to open his gift.
But he did not do so right away. He staved off the immediate
impulse to tear open the package in the first convenient dark
doorway beyond the church on the basis of his hunch that
people would be far more apt to buy a prettily wrapped item
late on a Christmas Eve than something in a plain box.

So he set off down Fifth Avenue with the unopened
package under his jacket to protect it from the falling snow.
From time to time he would stalk a solitary pedestrian. When
he'd succeed in attracting the person's attention, he'd say,
"Hey, Mister! You don't wanna buy a . . .?" and he would
thrust out the package. But before he ran out of words, the
pedestrian would have waved him off and passed on.

After awhile Jimmy found himself back at 42d Street.
He turned left toward Grand Central Station where, he hoped,
he might find some prospects among the late commuters and
holiday travelers.

At the entrance to the station he passed a green hut where
newspapers and magazines were being sold. The operator was
a small, heavily clothed man with a scarlet jaw overlaid with
a stubble of black beard. Around his waist he wore an apron
of coarse duckcloth, into which a long pocket had been sewn.
Inside nestled a bulge of change which the vender jingled
occasionally with cold and dirty hands.

Jimmy heard the sound of jostling pieces of silver and

115

nickel and copper. He stopped and looked enviously at the man. He found his look returned with a calculating stare. Clearly the newspaper man was a student of human nature, for he said to Jimmy at once, "Move along, buddy!"

For the next half hour Jimmy wandered through the cavernous sound of Grand Central Station — a sound made up of snatches of conversation, imperious declarations from unseen corners, dishes chinking together in an adjacent oyster bar, the clatter of train schedules being posted, and all held together by a long, hollow, unending echo in the key of A flat. It proved easy enough for Jimmy to approach people here. Still there were no buyers for his package. Only muttered demurrers. Only faces which became averted as Jimmy approached, and remained averted in spite of his entreaties.

In time Jimmy found that a tremor had taken control of his hands. He would have to make his sale very soon. If not, his hunger would take an ugly turn.

Finally an adolescent, who looked very much as though he were on his way home from prep school for the holidays, stopped to listen to what Jimmy had to say. He even took the package from Jimmy's hands and examined it as Jimmy spoke of a once-in-a-lifetime bargain.

"How much?" the boy asked.

"Ten," said Jimmy instead of the twenty he had meant to ask.

"Ten? Only ten? Hey, that's not half bad. What's inside?"

"It's worth a lot more than that," said Jimmy in a conspiratorial voice.

"Yeah," agreed the boy, shaking the package near his ear. "But what is it?"

116

"Buy it and find out," urged Jimmy, convinced by this time that he would have no difficulty making the sale.

"Hey!"

The boy now directed his voice toward a nearby bench. Jimmy saw that the boy was not alone. There were three cut from the same cloth seated nearby. Jimmy's hopes at once dissolved into the suspicion that he was being trifled with.

"Hey, listen to this!" the boy called out to his companions. "Here's a guy that's trying to sell me something, and he doesn't even know what it is! You know what *I* think? I think the guy swiped it or something!"

The boy's voice was purposely loud. It carried far beyond his three friends. As he spoke, his face broke into a mocking smile which emphasized an acne about the chin.

Jimmy grabbed for the package. The younger man whisked it out of reach.

To this Jimmy responded with a quiet dark threat which stunned the youth momentarily — long enough for Jimmy to take back his package. As he walked away, he was trailed by a chorus of insults and derisive laughter.

Jimmy now realized that he was being foolish in attempting to sell the package without knowing what was inside. He decided that the wisest course of action would be to go to the men's lavatory and open it there. He advised himself that a careful unwrapping would be required since, once he determined the contents, he wanted to rewrap the package as nicely as before.

As he turned a corner in one of the lower arcades of the terminal, Jimmy glimpsed at the far end of one passageway the entrance to the subway. The sight of it raised in his mind another possibility. Why not, he asked himself, go back to his own room and do the unwrapping and rewrapping there? Why not tend to this critical matter in a place where he would be safe? Besides, what better part of the city to sell the thing, whatever it was, than Greenwich Village? And if he couldn't sell it outright, he could always put it up for security on a small loan from any number of tradesmen he knew down there who weren't above a little loan-sharking on the side.

These new possibilities, bright and hopeful as the wrapping on the package, caused Jimmy to break into a slow, loping run. He passed through the outer doors leading to the subway, then made for the subway platform. Instead of entering through a coin turnstile, however, the penniless Jimmy pulled open an exit door on which the words "NO EN-TRANCE" had clearly been inscribed. Jimmy had used this method of avoiding paying the fare many times before. He found that all it took was a mixture of wariness and bravado. But on this night he possessed neither. And no sooner had he pulled open the barred door of that subway exit than he was collared from behind by a transit policeman.

"Not *that* way you don't, Mac!" the policeman told him, and he gave Jimmy a violent shove away from the door.

Jimmy looked at the policeman in bewilderment. For a moment he couldn't so much as understand what might be bothering him.

"Ya pay like anybody else!" the policeman told him. "Think you're a privileged character or sump'n?"

"I . . . I . . ." stuttered Jimmy.

"Go on! Get outta here!" said the policeman, obviously in no mood for back-talk. "If I catch you around here again, I'm gonna run you in!"

Jimmy lurched away. The rage which he summoned did not appear. All he managed, as he ascended the ramp which led to 42d Street, was the wistful hope that he might have better luck on 34th Street.

He walked south the eight blocks.

When he reached the next station, he found that he had become too unsure of himself to make another attempt on an exit door. He did not so much as bother to descend the steps which led to the subway level, but rather stood on the street above until there came to him the reverberating roar of an approaching train. It flooded the stairwell before him with sound, then broke off with the squeal of anguished metal. Jimmy heard the doors of the train roll back.

He turned, then, and began walking toward Greenwich Village.

The streets of the section of Manhattan through which he now began to pass were relatively deserted. This happened to be a commercial section of the city which on nights and weekends took on a vacant and foreboding character. It was an area of dark offices and dimly lighted hallways. The snow, which had begun to accumulate on streets and sidewalks, muffled what few noises there were. Jimmy had never before experienced Manhattan under such desolate circumstances.

After walking for several blocks, he happened upon a shaft of warm air emanating from a grate set in the sidewalk. He stopped and stood in it a moment, letting the rush of air warm him with a heat which smelled of soot and oiled electric motors. Then he walked on.

The tremor which had been hovering about him all evening was beginning to close in on him. His throat felt parched, and his head throbbed. Jimmy was approaching drug starvation and all that it implied. Only once before had he gone through the symptoms of withdrawal. It had been a brief episode. Brief and mild. But it imprinted on his memory the ominous indications of what total withdrawal might be. The prospect filled Jimmy with a vague dread. He quickened his pace.

A diner with steamed windows appeared out of the darkness. Through a patch of clear glass Jimmy caught sight of a man in a heavy leather jacket pressing a coffee cup against his lips with both hands.

Jimmy pressed on. Soon the lights of Union Square showed up ahead. This meant 14th Street and the northern approaches to the Village. Jimmy began counting the blocks between him and his room. Twelve . . . eleven . . . ten . . .

He was perspiring now, and yet shivering with cold. His feet plowed gouges in the snow. He could raise them no longer, could only shuffle along and let the snow cake over the toes of his shoes. Past the Chinese laundry he walked. Past the television repair shop with its opaque, brownish window and, on the far side, the graveyard of old television chassis and long-dead flies. Past the barbershop where one could get cheap haircuts. Past the drugstore on the corner.

He turned left. Along the side street he now took were parked cars sifted with snow. From somewhere came the sound of a shovel scraping the sidewalk.

Then the apartment house door was in front of him. He pulled it open and stepped inside. Passing the row of mail-boxes, Jimmy noticed a fold of paper resting diagonally in his. He reached for it. It turned out to be a rental notice. Stamped with red block letters across the face of the envelope were the words: PAST DUE.

"Thanks for the Christmas card, old buddy!" Jimmy shouted aloud in the empty hallway. "Thanks a lot!"

The saying of it brought on a brief spell of coughing. His throat felt as if it had been scraped raw.

Upstairs Jimmy found that the light in his room had been switched on. Someone, he realized, had rummaged through the place while he was away.

"Poor slob, if he thought he'd find anything *here*," Jimmy muttered aloud as he pushed the bureau against the door.

He sat down on the edge of the mattress and drew the package out from under his jacket.

As he examined it, there came to him the first uneasy feelings of doubt about the potential worth of what was contained in that package. These doubts had more to do with the wrapping than anything else. In the dim light of the church the wrapping had looked elegant. But now, under the glare of a plain light bulb, Jimmy could see that the paper only *looked* elegant. The embossments were not raised from the paper at all, but had only been cleverly imprinted. A few snowflakes had melted on the package and left tiny brown smudges behind. Along the edges of the package were indications that it had been ripped from a roll, and the ribbon could be seen not to be made out of cloth but of glossy paper fibers.

Jimmy shook the package. Whatever was inside, he thought, was certainly substantial enough. At least it wasn't a necktie or a handkerchief. There was something hard rattling around in there.

But how to get the paper off? Jimmy turned the package over and over, working out a strategy. He concluded that if he could just loosen the knot ever so slightly and slip the ribbon to one side, he could salvage the entire binding.

He began picking at the knot with his fingernails, only to find that his hands insisted on trembling. Besides, it was a tight knot, a perverse knot, all made up of stubborn broken strands.

There! At last it began to be worked free.

The paper, Jimmy noted, was further bound with several strips of cellophane tape. He attempted peeling one of the strips back, but the gum along the underside clung to the surface of the wrapping paper and lifted off a fine layer of the gold printing.

Jimmy fretted. This would not do!

He warmed the tape with his fingers, then began working it free from the edges. This procedure proved more successful. In a short time he had loosened the flaps at one end of the package. The others followed.

At last a single strip of tape along the center held the wrapping in place. Ever so carefully Jimmy removed it. He folded back the paper.

Underneath lay a pasteboard box. There was no inscription on it. Only an ill-stamped stock number.

The doubts returned. And he had been so *confident* about that package! After all, hadn't it been taken from one of the most stylish churches in Manhattan? He had felt all along that it ought to be good for 20 dollars at least! But now he wondered.

He stopped what he was doing and, for a moment, yearned for a reversal of time. He longed to be back outside that church once more. He wanted to experience once more the feeling of elation that had come to him as he had hurried down those church steps.

But already his thumb was pressing open the end of the box. He pulled the flap out and, without looking inside, aimed the open end of the box toward the bed.

Out onto the mattress slid the pink and blue mirror. Jimmy looked at it. He gaped at it. He stared at it in utter disbelief. His surprise was so intense that he could not seem to put things together—what it was he had here, or why he had it, or what he was supposed to be doing with it.

Then reality, like a deluge, broke over him and he laughed.

"Oh my God!" he yelped, and laughed again.

Then he groaned and rocked back and forth as though in pain.

"Oh no! Oh *no! Oh NO!*"

He laughed yet once more, and then bits of phrases began pouring out of his mouth. "And all the time . . . Oh my God! . . . And I thought . . . It's too funny . . . Too funny! . . . It's . . . it's . . . *hideous*! Oh my God, my *God! Look* at it! . . . It's awful! . . . I could almost throw up!"

Jimmy carried on like this for awhile, uncertain as to whether to give over to uncontrolled hilarity or rage. The latter finally prevailed. He clutched the mirror's handle with such force that his fingers whitened. It had become his intention to hurl the mirror against the wall with all his might. But before doing so, he wanted to lavish upon it all the misery and disappointment and pain in his soul, in the hope that in destroying the one, he would obliterate the other. So he began turning the mirror this way and that, hatred in his eyes, his lips drawn back in a snarl.

But then a certain question came along and quietly insinuated itself into the situation.

"*Who?*" he asked himself aloud. "Who in that filthy-rich church could have brought himself to buy something like *this*? Who could have brought himself to *give* something like this? Why . . . why, it must have been someone's idea of a joke," was the only explanation that occurred to him.

A joke! Of course! That was it. That was the only possibility! There could be no other! There simply *couldn't* be! Not when one considered the circumstances! Not when one considered that sea of mink and diamonds! It couldn't be anything but someone's idea of a practical joke!

Jimmy recalled the scene once more. With his inward eye he scanned the church. He visualized its half-filled pews. One by one he began a reexamination of its occupants. As in his memory he moved from one to another, he continued to find it impossible to believe that any one of them had actually bought, had actually purchased such an ugly mirror as this, had actually wrapped it in gift paper, had actually intended to give it to someone. And yet, he told himself, *someone* had! Someone there had bought the thing as a Christmas gift! Or a Christmas joke! But *who?* And *why?* It was a riddle which defied any solution!

And yet it came to him, finally, the solution, and pierced him. And the savage, sardonic rage left him to be replaced by a hollow hope that he might, after all, be wrong.

But no. He was *not* wrong. He knew that. As surely as he breathed he now knew who had bought this mirror.

"Remember? You wondered what he was doing there. You said to yourself that here was someone as out of place in that fancy church as you yourself, only it showed more on him. And he was sitting right about there. Yes, right where you picked up the package."

And, as Jimmy understood all this, there came to him yet one more insight like a hammerblow, for all at once he surmised why the mirror had been bought, and for whom, and what it must have meant to the buyer to be able to give it, and what it must have cost in a self-denying hoard of pennies and nickels.

"Oh no," Jimmy said softly.

He slumped over. And the pity he had felt for himself became transformed into compassion for a boy who had entered a strange church to warm himself only to be robbed.

"Oh no," Jimmy said once more. He turned the mirror over in his hand. The glass came up and showed him his own face. He looked at it. It seemed almost strange to him. He wondered if this were really the face which day after day he presented to others.

"So this is what you've come to," he told the reflection.

He lay back against the mattress and longed to weep. But instead there came, in a gathering fury, the first convulsions of withdrawal.

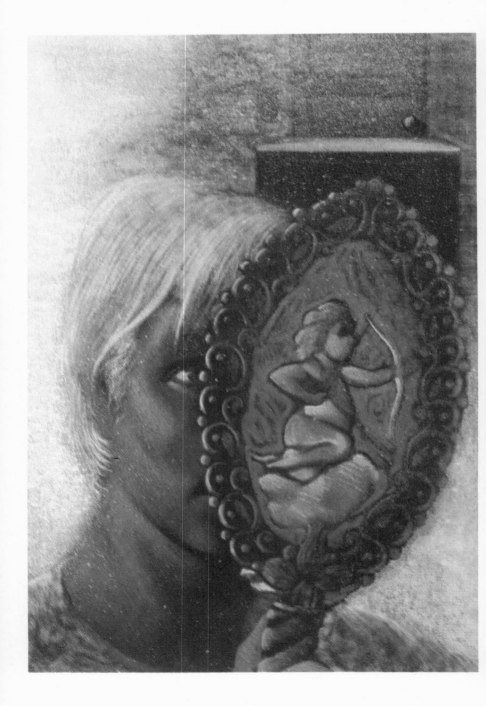

THE SECOND GIFT

Rosie arrived home very late. His mother greeted him with a mixture of relief and exasperation. She took the wrapped package from his hand and laid it under their tree — emaciated affair that it was, with a total of 10 lonely Christmas lights, as many decorations, and a meager, uneven distribution of tinsel.

Rosie was given a bath. He was scrubbed and soaped and brushed and wiped until he fairly gleamed, and all of this to the accompaniment of a great many sighings and wonderings what he would ever come to. Then he was given a cup of cocoa, an apple, and a piece of bread, and afterwards packed into bed with a kiss.

Rosie slept lightly and nervously at first. In years past he had often stayed awake wondering what gifts *he* might receive on the morrow. Now, for the first time in his life, he was about to learn that the role of giver contains ever so much more anxiety than that of receiver.

However, after a good many pleasant anticipations of his mother's reaction to his gift, he fell, at last, into a deep slumber. When he next opened his eyes, it was light outside.

He found his mother in the small kitchen surrounded by his two sisters who, at the moment, were chattering away like chipmunks. Outside on a fire escape railing Rosie saw a solitary starling, feathers puffed against the gray cold, looking toward the window with a great many nods and tilts of the head.

"Merry Christmas, Rosie," said his mother in her soft way.

"Merry Christmas," replied Rosie importantly.

"Did Rosie get spanked, Ma?" asked the older of his two sisters.

"No I din't, you dumb," said Rosie indignantly.

"You *said* you would," the little girl accused her mother.

"Eat your cereal!" replied Mrs. Sims mildly. She turned to her son. "Do you want egg, Roosevelt?"

"Just cereal. . . . When we gonna open the presents?"

"Just as soon as you're done with breakfast," said his mother.

The spoon flashed, and Rosie's cheeks expanded while his jaws made frantic efforts to keep pace with the intake.

Afterwards at the tree Rosie said, "Mom, you open yours first."

"No," she said. "I open mine *last!*"

For Rosie's younger sister there was a Raggedy Ann doll, a toy iron, a small xylophone with colored bars, an orange-colored dress with matching hair ribbons, and a 29 cents box of chocolate nonpareils from Rosie.

For the other sister there was a baby carriage — which Rosie's mother had spent hours assembling, having been obliged to use a table knife as a screw driver, a game of pick-up-sticks, a pink sweater with gold sequins, a tin of water-colors, and a box of nonpareils like her sister's.

Rosie got a pair of trousers with a plaid belt attached, a toy telescope, a book about the Hardy Boys, a pair of sun-glasses, and a real leather wallet.

For Rosie, however, this was all preliminary, since, as previously noted, it is not only more blessed to give than to receive; it is also more nerve-wracking. He barely savored his own gifts. And he grew quite shrill, indeed unpleasant, in urging his sisters to open theirs faster.

At last there was but one package under the tree. It was, if nothing else, the most prettily wrapped of them all — all gold, both ribbon and paper together.

As Rosie handed the package to his mother, she said with exaggerated curiosity, "Now what could *this* be?"

Rosie could not bear to watch the great event. Being a very small boy, it had never occurred to him that the act of giving might have certain painful aspects. He had given his mother gifts before — gifts made in school out of construction paper and crayon and white paste — but never had he truly understood what this business of giving was all about. Not until this year. Before it had been a species of politeness. A reciprocation. A this for that.

But this year his experience of giving had come to assume mysterious, otherworldly dimensions, a fact due in no small part to the measure of his own self-investment. There had been the months of preparation. There had been the allowance money put carefully away. There had been the nights when he'd been kept awake by anticipation. Then, at last, there had been that long and dangerous journey for just the right gift. All this he'd undertaken simply so he could place a gift in the hands of one for whom he felt a quite unequivocal love. And the net result? At the moment it was little more than an uncomfortable and mounting anxiety which turned on giving's ultimate question: Will the gift be accepted? Will it be taken and cherished? Will it be made one's own?

In anticipation of its answer, Rosie found he could not watch. All he could manage was an inspection of the floor and a listening to the rustle of paper and the excited murmurs of his sisters.

The rustling at last ceased, and there followed a brief silence.

Then he heard his mother say, "It's very nice, Rosie."

Looking up, Rosie saw — well, he didn't see what he *expected* to see. He didn't see that beautiful mirror he had so carefully picked out. No indeed. What met his astonished gaze was something quite different. There seemed to be a *necklace* dangling from his mother's hand.

"Very, very pretty," his mother was saying, and into her voice there crept a suggestion of merriment. It was almost as if the gift had somehow amused her so much that it was all she could do to keep from laughing out loud. And Rosie, sensitized to his mother's response, caught its innuendo and bristled angrily.

"What's that?" Rosie heard himself saying, as he was still a bit nonplussed.

"It's what you gave me," said his mother. "And it's very nice, she added with an effort at conviction, all the while wondering how she could keep from actually wearing such a flamboyant example of counter jewelry without hurting her son's feelings. Perhaps, she advised herself, she could wear it at home evenings.

"I din't give you *that!* " said Rosie, coming closer.

"It was in the package, Rosie," replied his mother.

"Then the girl give me the wrong one," said Rosie in a strangled voice.

"*Gave*," said his mother. "*Gave* you the wrong one . . .

It doesn't matter, Rosie. It's very pretty. I like it very much."

"But I got you a *mirra*," explained Rosie, his voice elevating a few pitches. "I got you a pretty mirra, and she give me the wrong one. I din't give you no necklace," he said in a trembling high voice.

"But it's very nice," said his mother consolingly, and she smiled at her daughters who, by this time, were awaiting open-mouthed the irreversible onset of a scene.

"I din't give you no necklace! I give you a mirra," Rosie insisted, and he looked with distaste on the object held out toward him by his mother for their mutual approval.

"But can't you see how pretty it is?" she said, and with a motion of her hand invited him to hold it and see for himself.

"No!" shouted Rosie, "no, no! No! NO! *NO!*" — each "no" louder than the one before, and with a lunge he grabbed the necklace from his mother's hand and threw it across the room. The necklace hit the floor with a thwack and skidded under a bed. The sound of the skid gave over to a silence, then to a few muffled preliminary sobs from Rosie. Then he wept bitterly.

"Now Rosie, don't you mind," said his mother. "It's the thought that counts. What matter if it's a mirror or a necklace? It's the love back of it, son. I know how far you went for that present, Rosie. I know how you got yourself cold and hungry for me. That's the *real* gift, Roosevelt! The rest don't matter so much. What difference if it's a mirror or a necklace?"

Her words only caused Rosie to weep louder.

"Besides," she continued, poking at the remains of the package with her fingers, "look here! It was wrapped so nicely! Such nice paper! Such nice ribbon! How many mothers get such a pretty package? And it even came in a nice case . . . ."

There was a name engraved on the case in a fine script. Rosie's mother held it close to her eyes.

"Look here, Rosie! It says it's from . . . it's from . . . from . . . *Rosie!*" cried Mrs. Sims. *"Where did you get this box?"*

Rosie continued to cry.

"Roosevelt Sims!" she declared in a no-nonsense manner. "I said where did you get this box?"

"Store," said Rosie, momentarily startled out of his crying.

"Store? *What* store? Only one store like this, and they wouldn't let any little boy from Harlem in the front door! Roosevelt Sims! You look at your mam and tell her that you didn't buy this from some man on the street!"

"No, mama," said Rosie.

"Then what kind of store was it, Rosie? Tell me the truth now!"

"Just a store," said Rosie, and he made an effort at crying again, but failed.

"A big store?"

"Sorta."

"How much did you pay for it?"

"I'm not s'pposed to tell."

"Rosie!"

"Two dollah."

"Roosevelt Sims! Look me in the eye and promise me that you bought this in a store for two dollars!"

"Honest!"

"Get it for me!"

Rosie crawled under the bed, retrieved the necklace,

132

and brought it to his mother. She took the necklace, examined it closely, held it up to the light. Then she moaned softly, "Oh Lord! And how am I gonna raise 'em if I'm far away in jail?"

For the next hour and more, Rosie told and retold the details of his trip to Fifth Avenue. Every step, every turn, every breath practically, was described again and again. Rosie claimed over and over that he could not be sure of the exact location of the store, though he felt he could find it again if he had to.

Finally Rosie's mother told him that the first thing they would do the next morning would be to go to the store whose name had been imprinted on the necklace case. She told Rosie that he would have to tell the truth to the people there, even if it meant that all of them would be shut up in prison for a hundred thousand years. And Rosie promised to do so with solemn and somewhat confused eyes.

Having extracted this promise, Rosie's mother declared that if jail it was going to be, Christmas still came first. And this meant a trip to Aunt Mary's.

One other matter. Since the necklace would be far safer with her than left in the apartment, and since, one way or another, it had been her son's gift — why, the only proper thing to do was to wear it.

And this is exactly what she did, even though it meant clutching the necklace to her breast throughout the entire train ride to Jersey City for fear that the clasp would give way.

It was a splendid Christmas. There seemed no end of relatives and friends and laughter and punch and cake and candy at Aunt Mary's.

And if Rosie's mother did not receive many compliments on her necklace, as it caught the light from a thousand angles and turned it into ten thousand fires and made her seem the princess of an exotic kingdom, it may have been because most of the people there wondered what had brought such a quiet and dignified woman to wear such a gaudy arrangement of what was obviously fake jewelry.

THE THIRD GIFT

And what is to be made of the third gift given on that Christmas Eve? For make no mistake, three gifts were given on that hallowed night. Even though the casual eye might account for only two, there were actually three gifts — three conferred and three received by three separate and distinct individuals.

But how does one describe the third gift? How does one explain a gift which has neither shape nor weight nor substance? How, in these materialistic times, does one bestow credibility on a gift which cannot be seen or heard or touched?

Perhaps, once you think about it, there just *isn't* any way. Perhaps we can only say that it is quite impossible to contain that third gift. Perhaps we must admit that the last gift in our catalog is too incalculable to be reduced to a set of perceivable dimensions, too vast to be confined in a box and wrapped in gilt paper and bound with a pretty ribbon.

And yet, for all its boundless character, a gift it remained. And it must be further stated, without any equivocation whatsoever, that Helen Pierson Lockroy bore her gift from that church just as surely as Rosie and Jim Mortimer bore theirs. It had become hers by will and deed, even though she wasn't entirely aware of the fact at that time. Indeed, it wouldn't be until many years later that she would come to realize what a priceless gift had been conferred upon her that

Christmas Eve at the very moment she began behaving in such an impetuous and foolish manner.

So the gift was hers. Hers without any qualification or reservation. Hers whether she knew it or not. And hers it would remain until the end of her days. And this is how she opened it.

After the bus containing Rosie had pulled away from the curb, Helen Lockroy walked a few blocks in the direction of her apartment, then beckoned to a cab and rode the rest of the way home. She inquired en route about the cab driver's family and was given a rambling discourse in return. When the time came, she added a generous tip to the fare. "For the children," she explained, and made for the door of her apartment house before the cab driver could reply. Leonard, the night doorman, greeted her in his usual frosty manner, and looked almost surprised at the warmth of her reply. Then she chatted with the elevator man all the way to her floor.

After she closed the door to her apartment, she stopped for a moment, astonished by her actions. It wasn't like her to behave so casually with cab drivers and apartment staff! She wondered why *she* should care whether they had a merry Christmas and a happy New Year or not, then dismissed the question as utterly ridiculous. She cared. Cared a great deal, in fact. And that was an end to it.

Astonishment soon gave over to fatigue. The events of the evening had exhausted her. She went directly to bed and for the first time in many years was granted a deep, dreamless slumber. When she awakened, it was nearing eight o'clock. She felt within her an unusual gnawing pain, which she soon diagnosed as nothing more dangerous than a healthy hunger.

137

She decided then and there that she would scramble a few eggs for breakfast.

Later, when she had fixed herself a second cup of coffee, she sipped it by the window as she watched the heads of holiday pedestrians below.

It occurred to her after awhile that it was time to set out a few of the Christmas decorations that had been stored away for more years than she could remember. As she removed them from their cardboard boxes and dusted them off, she found herself once again remembering former Christmases. Yet, for reasons still unknown to her, the memory of them did not bring the usual pain. Her remembrance of childhood, of the poignant years of youth, of marriage and motherhood, of the long somnolent autumn of middle years — all of this seemed like a story too beautiful and too unique to be told. And yet somehow, on this Christmas morning, it all seemed inconsequential too, like a carving in ice. The significance of life, she realized, lay somewhere else, lay somewhere beyond the scraps and tatters of memory by which she comprehended it. And although she could not be entirely certain what that significance was, she felt that it lay very close to what happens when people care for one another and give to each other.

As the noon hour approached, she was reminded of a certain duty she was obliged to attend to on this day. She walked over to the escritoire, sat down, took out a sheet of note paper, then proceeded to stare off into space for fully 10 minutes before setting down a word.

The letter she eventually wrote went as follows:

Dear Mr. Barnswallow:

First let me wish you a Merry Christmas, for I write this letter on the 25th and, since I shall send it to you by messenger, you should receive it on this day as well (that is, unless you are out of town, and I do so hope you are not).

Before reading any further, let me warn you that what follows might strike you as a bit odd. Indeed, you may think the time has come for me to be committed to one of those institutions for senile old ladies. At any rate, I hope not. I want you to know that I feel perfectly fine, and am no more forgetful than I ever was, of which, as you well know, the less said the better.

Perhaps, before reading what follows, it would be best if you remind yourself that it is one of the duties of the attorneys of rich old ladies to indulge the idiosyncrasies of their clients, and to do so with the customary discretion. I hope that you understand me, and at the same time will continue to be my friend, for this is how I have always thought of you primarily.

As you were apparently informed yesterday afternoon, on a sudden whim I arranged the purchase of an extremely expensive diamond and emerald necklace. I gather that you arranged its insurance, and I have no doubt that you did so with your usual efficiency.

Now I must surprise you with the fact that yesterday evening, again on a whim, I gave that necklace away. Yes, *gave it away*, Mr. Barnswallow. And not only that, I gave the necklace to neither friend nor relative. The truth of it is that I gave it to a perfect stranger.

I can picture you reading this and supposing that I have taken utter *leave* of my senses, and I doubt that the circumstances surrounding this act will dissuade you. Nevertheless, I find myself obliged to tell you of them anyway. The stranger happened to be a young boy who was seated close to me in church. He left his place for a short time and, while he was gone, a sneak thief stole a Christmas package

139

which belonged to him. I witnessed the theft, but was unable to prevent it. Earlier I had noticed that the boy's package and my own were of similar size and wrapping. So I simply put mine where the other had been.

Curiously, this exchange seemed more foolish to me then than it does now. I shall not tax your imagination with trying to explain why. I inform you only so that you may prepare for the practical consequences to follow.

It occurs to me that two parties need to be told of my actions, which is to say the jewelry concern and the insurers. Please inform both of my desire that this matter be handled in total confidence. I would be ever so mortified if news of this affair were to get into the hands of the press.

As to the rest of it, here are my instructions. In the event that the necklace has disappeared forever, the insurers should be told that I shall not, and quite rightly, enter any claim against them.

If, however, the necklace be returned to the store through some underworld channel, you may inform the firm that I shall redeem the necklace for whatever price seems right to them.

I have a feeling, somehow, that neither of these possibilities shall come to pass. The lad to whom I gave the necklace seemed to me (I don't know why!) a very honest little boy, and I have every confidence that he will show up at the store in the company of an older person — his father, perhaps, or an older brother — to return the necklace.

If this should happen, *if,* mind you, a lad by the name of Roosevelt Sims or one of his representatives appears at the jewelry firm to return the necklace, would you see that he is courteously received and given a thorough explanation of how the packages came to be switched. This should be done — need I say so again? — anonymously. After explaining the circumstances, the lad is to be told that my gift stands. No strings, Mr. Barnswallow!

But, oh yes! You might have the person doing the explaining tell the lad that while he is free to do whatever he likes with his gift, the person who gave it would like to suggest—*suggest,* Mr. Barnswallow, not *demand*—that should the store offer a good price for the repurchase of the necklace, young Mr. Sims might be reminded that a good education is every bit as precious as emeralds and diamonds.

I trust that you will carry out this unusual mission without delay. I send my Christmas regards to Mrs. Barnswallow.

Sincerely,
Helen Pierson Lockroy

As she waited for the messenger to arrive, her attention was drawn to an address book lying in one of the cubbyholes of the desk. Without quite knowing why, Mrs. Lockroy drew forth the address book and began idly leafing through the pages. Many of the names, she noted, were of people who had died years ago and had never been crossed off. Here was a job, she told herself, that must be taken care of before long.

In the process of turning the pages, she came upon one which was blank save for a telephone number scribbled at an angle from one corner to the other. The number had been underlined. At its end stood a half dozen large exclamation points. The writing she recognized as her husband's. Nor could there be any doubt about the number. It was the one he had used to reach Vivian before he died.

As she gazed at that number written down so long ago, written in a manner so obviously designed to attract her attention, she found herself wondering if her daughter had the number still. She glanced in the direction of Elwood's chair as if seeking confirmation.

The chair stood there quite empty. She knew, as she looked at it, that Elwood would never again return to sit in it. He was gone now, gone as completely as her past was gone, gone as surely as her former correspondents were gone. But, for all that, she could almost feel his encouragement — palpable, insistent. "Go ahead, Helen!" he seemed to be saying. "Call her up and ask how she's been! She'd be so happy if you did!"

Still Helen Lockroy delayed. Giving away the necklace seemed the merest trifle compared to this. But then a whimsical thought chanced along with the suggestion that Vivian might be lonely on this Christmas Day. And that was why, without a moment's hesitation, she picked up the receiver and began to dial.